The look

misery.

"Oh, hell, Lina," he said and rose, pulling her to her feet and into his arms. For a moment she stood stiff. He was about to release her when she made a muffled sound, leaned on him and seemed to go boneless. They stood like that for a long time. Inhaling her scent, he cradled the back of her head with one hand while he held her up with his other arm.

The hard mound of her belly felt odd wedged between them. It was like a purse or a—no, not a basketball—a soccer ball. Maybe one of those kid-sized ones. Then he had the dazed thought that what he felt between them wasn't kid-sized—it *was* a kid. A whole, complete person in the making.

The fact that this particular baby might be his was something he couldn't let himself think about, not yet.

Dear Reader,

As you may have noticed by now, I have a thing about men who have trouble admitting to the softer emotions. Of course, many of my heroes are cops, who have to be tough guys. How else can they protect themselves from the awful things they see every day? But honestly, as with so many of the themes I come back to over and over, I suspect this one has to do with my own family and childhood.

I remember meeting my paternal grandfather, who was probably a good man but was cold enough to make you shiver. I'm willing to bet that man never in his life told a woman he loved her, never mind his two sons. Dad grew up in the Depression in the worst of poverty, his mother an invalid, his father trying to keep them together. Result: a man who cared deeply, but had a really hard time issuing compliments or saying such simple words as *I love you*. Dad has been gone for fifteen years now, but I still sometimes think I hear his truck coming down the hill to my house. He'd show up, mow my lawn or clean my gutters, and leave, sometimes even without stopping in the house to say hi. But I always knew that was love in action.

My heroine in this book, Lina Jurick, was betrayed by a man once and doesn't know how to trust Bran Murphy, emotionally remote. I hope you enjoy their struggle—his to accept what he feels and articulate it, hers to understand that love can be expressed in many ways.

Janice Kay Johnson

JANICE KAY JOHNSON

The Baby He Wanted

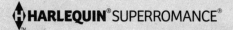

HARLEQUIN®SUPERROMANCE®

Recycling programs
for this product may
not exist in your area.

ISBN-13: 978-0-373-60956-7

The Baby He Wanted

Copyright © 2016 by Janice Kay Johnson

Printed in U.S.A.

www.Harlequin.com

An author of more than ninety books for children and adults, **Janice Kay Johnson** writes about love and family—about the way generations connect and the power our earliest experiences have on us throughout life. An eight-time finalist for a Romance Writers of America RITA® Award, she won a RITA® Award in 2008 for her Harlequin Superromance novel *Snowbound*. A former librarian, Janice raised two daughters in a small town north of Seattle, Washington.

Books by Janice Kay Johnson

Visit the Author Profile page at Harlequin.com.

CHAPTER ONE

COMPANY OF ANY kind wasn't on Bran Murphy's mind when he walked into the tavern. His plan was to find a stool at the bar well away from anyone else.

But there she was, sitting alone, with hair the color of dark honey laced with sunbeams flowing in waves down her back.

He let his gaze pause on her only briefly before he scanned the entire room. As with most cops, looking for trouble had become automatic. He didn't spot any tonight. A local country band played a ballad and three couples shuffled on the small dance floor. A crowd hooted and called good-natured insults around the pool tables. People seemed to be having a good time.

He locked onto her.

She'd chosen to sit at one end of the bar, six stools separating her from the closest patron, a man hunched morosely over his drink. Completely still, she looked even more alone than the physical distance suggested. Her head was bent and she seemed to be gazing into her drink as if the glass held tea leaves that would reveal arcane secrets.

Nothing about her suggested that she sought companionship. Giving in to impulse for the second time tonight, Bran took the stool only one away from hers anyway.

She glanced his way, giving him a glimpse of a perfect oval face and gray-green eyes filled with grief or anger, he couldn't be sure. Then she went back to pondering the mixed drink she hadn't touched.

"Are you all right?" he asked, even though he hadn't walked in here with any intention of being sociable, either. In fact, he didn't know why he *was* here. He should have stopped at the store for a bottle of whiskey or a couple of six-packs of dark beer and gotten stinking drunk in the privacy of his apartment. But the first impulse of the evening, a sudden one, had made him turn into the tavern parking lot instead.

Hell, maybe this was smarter. He wouldn't let himself get so drunk he couldn't drive home, which meant he wouldn't feel quite so shitty come morning.

On his wedding day.

"I'm not sick, if that's what you mean," the blonde said, softly enough he had to lean toward her to hear.

Bran signaled the bartender, ordering a pitcher instead of the whiskey he'd intended.

Looked like he had something in common with the blonde. Sure as hell, neither of them was here to celebrate.

He nodded his thanks for the pitcher and poured himself a glass, then took a swallow.

"You want to talk about it?"

She gave that some thought before answering. "No." This time she studied him. "If you're planning to hit on me, you're wasting your time."

"Hadn't crossed my mind," he told her, although that wasn't entirely true. No, it hadn't, but it would have eventually, and now that the subject had been introduced, his mind stuck on it.

"Oh. Okay," she said.

Damn, she was beautiful. Her tan was more pale gold than brown, her nose small, her mouth pretty… Skinny jeans molded to slim legs that he thought might prove to be reasonably long. Well-rounded hips and generous breasts suggested she had a genuine hourglass figure. Bran liked curves.

Paige hadn't had many of those.

She went to the gym almost daily, determined to pare every hint of extra flesh from her body. As the wedding approached, she'd become fanatical about her diet and exercise, striving for some notion of perfection that wasn't his. He'd given up reasoning with her. In fact, he hadn't had much chance, since wedding preparations made her even more unavailable than she'd already been.

Paige wasn't here. A beautiful blonde was.

As he watched, she finally picked up her glass and guzzled what looked like a mixed drink as if it was water and she was parched. A shudder went through her before she plunked the glass down on the polished bar.

The bartender, a balding guy in his forties, appeared. "You want another one? Whiskey sour, right?"

"Yes, please."

Her choice suggested she wasn't much of a drinker.

Bran was on his second glass when the band began another ballad. Out of the corner of his eye, he saw the dance floor empty.

"Would you like to dance?" he asked.

The blonde blinked as if she was having trouble bringing him into focus, but her voice sounded clear. "Okay."

She slid off the bar stool and into his arms as if she belonged there. She might be five foot six, he guessed, which made his shoulder a perfect resting place for her head.

He barely moved his feet. Mostly, they swayed. He didn't press her as close as he would have liked, figuring it wouldn't be gentlemanly, given that he had a serious hard-on. Bran closed his eyes and rested his cheek against her head, inhaling a familiar scent that threw him back a lot of years. Mint.

A patch of the plant had grown beside the back steps of his childhood home. Even brushing the leaves was enough to awaken the fragrance. His mom used to make a sweetened drink with orange and lemon juice, orange peels and mint leaves pulled from that plant.

Until this moment, he'd forgotten all about that drink and how much he loved it. Twenty-five years was a long time.

He nuzzled the honey-colored hair, as smooth and luxuriously textured as heavy satin. The woman in his arms moved her head a little, as if she was rubbing her cheek against him. She gave a small sigh that shot straight to his groin.

The last notes of the song died, but neither of them moved for a minute. Finally, reluctantly, he released her. Her hands slid down his chest and she stepped back, shy.

Back on their bar stools, he said, "I'm Bran. Short for Brandon." He held out a hand.

She slowly extended her much smaller, fine-boned hand. "Lina. Short for Alina."

"Lina." He liked that. "Well, Lina, what do you usually do for fun?"

She crinkled her nose. "Not this. Um… I'm a huge reader. Movies are fine, but usually I'd rather read."

He smiled. "Me, too."

"Really?" She brightened, her expression almost…hopeful.

He felt strange for a minute, as if his heart had contracted, briefly depriving him of oxygen. His voice came out husky when he said, "Really. A lot of nonfiction. Mysteries and thrillers, anything random that grabs me."

She liked mysteries, too. They compared authors, then argued about a few books one of them had loved and the other hated. She suggested an author he hadn't tried, and he did the same. Eventually, they segued to movies, then music. She swam laps three or four times a week at the high school pool, she told him, and admitted to having been on a youth team and her high school team.

She made a face. "I'm not built to be fast, though."

His gaze dropped to her breasts, and his blood headed south again. As far as he could see, she was built just right.

They slow danced a couple more times. Lina didn't seem any more interested in line dancing than he did.

She had a couple more drinks. He finished his

pitcher but figured he was still—barely—safe to drive, given how long he'd been working on it.

When the bartender came to offer her another refill, Bran shook his head. Lina scowled at him. "Why'd you do that?"

"Honey, you're sloshed."

"I'm not your honey." She slipped off the stool and wobbled, grabbing it to restore her balance. "Not anyone's honey."

He was glad to hear that. "You planning to drive home?"

"Don't know."

"You're not." He took out his wallet and tossed down enough bills to cover both their drinks. "I can call you a taxi, or drive you home."

Her eyes narrowed. "How come you're not shlosh...*sloshed*, too?"

"I'm bigger than you. I can drink more without getting hit as hard." When he stood, his head swam, but his balance was okay. He wrapped an arm around her, gratified when hers slipped around his waist and she leaned into him.

"'Kay," she murmured.

They stepped outside into a too-warm June night. A slap of cold air would have felt good. Bran looked around the now-crowded parking lot in perplexity, unable to remember where he had left his Camaro.

He had keys, he knew he did. He patted his pocket. There they were. Just no car.

The neon sign right across the road from the tavern drew his eye. Motel. Vacancy. The "No" part was turned off. As lodging went, it was pretty basic, but decent as far as he knew. It wasn't on the sheriff's department radar for drug dealing or prostitution, at least.

"We should get a room," he decided.

"No hitting on me. You said."

"I changed my mind," he admitted. "But if you just want to sleep, that's what we'll do."

"I changed my mind, too," she confided in a small, husky voice.

Rocketed to full arousal that easily, he steered her across the road into the motel office, where a bored kid who looked to be barely of legal age swiped Bran's credit card and asked for a signature.

Bran took the key—yes, a real key—as well as the card with their room number on it and collected Lina from the chair where he'd parked her.

The flight of outside stairs was a challenge, but they made it, Lina giggling as he tried to jam the key in the lock. Hell, he *was* drunk. Sloshed. Plowed. It worried him that she was, too. Did this qualify as taking advantage of her?

The key finally turned and he pushed the door open. He all but fell in. Lina giggled again.

Oh, yeah, she was drunk.

She closed the door behind them and flipped a switch that turned on lamps on each side of the queen-size bed. Bran stood, doing battle with his conscience.

"Will you kiss me?" Lina asked timidly.

He cleared his throat. "I'd like to kiss you. But Lina… Are you going to be sorry in the morning?"

He waited, suspended in fear that she'd come to her senses now. Of course she would. She wasn't a one-night-stand kind of woman. But, *God*, he hoped she wouldn't change her mind.

Little worried lines formed on her forehead as she scrutinized his face. "You won't hurt me, will you?"

"No!" He framed her face in hands that shook with an unfamiliar tremor. "Never." He hesitated. "I'm a cop, Lina."

"Oh." She nibbled uncertainly on her lower lip as her eyes continued to search his. "Do you have, um, you know? A condom? Because I don't. And I'm not on anything."

"I do. I have a couple in my wallet."

Paige had refused to go on the pill or a birth control patch until after the wedding. *Didn't he know how all those hormones made women gain weight? No way was she messing with her body right now!* Bran had really hated the necessity of wearing a condom, but right this minute, he didn't want to think about how he'd have felt if he hadn't had one.

Lina laid a hand on his shoulder and rose onto tiptoe. "Then I won't be sorry," she murmured, and brushed her mouth over his.

The kiss exploded. He drove his fingers into that mass of silky hair, tilting her head until he found the perfect angle. Her arms came around his neck and he closed one hand over her bottom, lifting and pressing her against him. That fast, his hips rocked. He had to have her *now*.

Their clothes flew. T-shirts first, which caused her to start kissing and stroking his chest. Desperate, he found the catch on her bra and released the most beautiful breasts he'd ever seen. He propelled her backward until she came up against the bed, then lifted her and laid her down, his mouth capturing a nipple before her back hit the mattress. He licked and teased until she gripped his head and repeated, "Please, please, please." And then he suckled. The little noises she made had him groaning and pulling back.

He told her how beautiful she was while he yanked off her boots and peeled tiny panties and stretchy jeans off her curvaceous hips and down those long legs.

For a second, one knee planted on the bed between her thighs, Bran stopped just to look. He had never even imagined a woman as sexy as this one. Her body was both delicate and voluptuous, her lips puffy from his kisses, her eyes heavy-lidded. And then there was that richly colored hair, masses of it spread across the bedspread. The disconcerting idea struck him that she also looked vulnerable. If she hadn't been drunk, she'd be grabbing for something to cover herself.

He reared back to kick off his shoes and un-button his jeans. Lucky he'd gone into the tavern unarmed, rare for him. His gun was locked in a safe beneath the driver's seat of his Camaro. A tavern parking lot wasn't the best place to leave an expensively restored vintage sports car…but damn…he'd never wanted anything in his life the way he did this woman.

His jeans fit so tightly at the moment, he emptied his pockets onto the dresser top before he cautiously unzipped. Jeans and boxers gone, he pulled out the couple condoms from the wallet, tossing one packet onto the bedside table and ripping open the second one. His hands were still shaking. He lifted his gaze to see that she had risen up onto her elbows and was staring with an expression that did amazing things to his ego. A blush rose on her cheeks even as her tongue came out to touch her lips.

He got the condom on and crawled forward until he could kiss her again, voraciously this time.

He bypassed her glorious breasts and splayed a hand on her belly, circling until his fingers encountered the nest of curls the same honey shade as her hair and just as silky.

She was already so wet, his finger slid between her folds and right into her. She cried out and grabbed his arms.

"Now. Please, now."

He stroked her for another few seconds, the limit of his self-control, before he spread her thighs and thrust deep.

She looked at him in astonishment and whispered, "Oh," after which her eyes closed and she tipped her head back.

Considerate was beyond him. Bran couldn't have gone slow if he'd had a gun to his head. He set a hard, fast rhythm that she matched, clutching at him as her hips rose and fell. He couldn't have stopped the orgasm that lifted him like a monster wave and swept him forward, either. But she cried out at the same time, her tiny convulsions part of the staggering pleasure.

THEY MADE LOVE twice more. In the middle of the night, Lina had come back from the bathroom to find him awake, waiting for her.

This morning, she'd slid out of an amazing dream to find it had been real. A man's hard body spooned her. His erection pressed against her butt and his fingers played between her legs.

She groaned and arched convulsively. He gave a low, husky laugh and closed his teeth on the bundle of muscle and nerves that ran between her neck and shoulder. Then he lifted her leg and slid into her. It felt…amazing. Unlike the night's tumultuous lovemaking, this time he moved lazily, teasing her by not going as deep as she craved. His fingers circled and pressed until she heard her own small, broken cries.

Suddenly, he groaned, half lifted her to her knees, and drove hard and fast. She came by the third stroke, taking him with her.

They both collapsed. After a moment, he groaned.

"Now, *that's* how I like to wake up."

Lina hadn't known it was possible to wake up to anything like that. "It was…really good." She wasn't even sure she was 100 percent awake. An awareness that she felt queasy suggested she was. Nothing like a hangover to ground her.

"I need a shower," he said, kissed her nape and pushed himself out of bed.

She heard him gathering his clothes from the floor, but didn't roll over. She hadn't even seen his face yet this morning. Lina closed her eyes, glad at least that she could picture him. Big, solid, broad-shouldered. His dark auburn hair had been disheveled. Her fingers remembered how silky that hair was. His face was all male, but too rough-hewn to be handsome. It was his bright blue eyes, sharp, that had captivated her. Now she wondered what he'd seen when he looked at her. Had he known from the beginning that she could be coaxed into bed?

She moaned. God, what had she done? How stupid was this, getting drunk and checking into a cheap motel for a one-night stand with a guy she'd met at a tavern? A guy whose last name she didn't even know?

Really, really stupid, that's what.

Worse yet, she couldn't help wondering if she had half intended to do just this. Why else had she gone to the tavern? She could have gotten drunk at home.

The shower came on. Lina rolled to her back and covered her eyes with her hands. She had to have been desperate for confirmation that she was an attractive woman. There was no other explanation for her idiocy. Finding out that David had cheated on her had damaged her self-esteem as much as her heart.

The divorce had been finalized in December. *Merry Christmas to me.*

She would have said she was over him until she was hit by yesterday's nugget of news about

David and his new wife. Now she couldn't even kid herself that he'd ever loved her.

Still…sex with a stranger in a seedy motel room?

He hadn't felt like a stranger by the time he kissed her. He'd felt like a guy she had really liked. They had things in common. He seemed… decent. Not to mention sexy. He'd given her an out, and she believed he'd have accepted a *no* if she'd said it.

A funny sensation blossomed in her chest, pushing out the shame. Hope? Yes, hope. Maybe he'd really liked her, too. Maybe this wasn't as sleazy as it seemed.

Please, God, she thought.

Deciding she needed to be dressed when he reappeared, Lina slipped out of bed and saw that he'd laid her clothes neatly on the dresser as he picked up his own. Which meant he was considerate, too.

Her first clue that she'd screwed up majorly was the icky feeling that she was leaking between her legs. Something was running down the inside of her thighs.

Panic squeezed her. Oh, God. He'd used a condom the first two times they'd…not made love… had sex. But not this morning. She had the awful memory of him tossing a single packet on the bedside stand while tearing open the other one.

He hadn't had three.

"That *bastard.*"

Lina calculated quickly. It was late enough in the month, she should be safe—unless he took strange women he picked up in bars to motels on a regular basis and didn't use condoms.

Her chest felt horribly tight and she was all but panting for breath. Get dressed. That was what she had to do next.

In the act of reaching for her clothes, she saw everything he'd left on the dresser top. A wallet, a set of car keys, a Harris County Sheriff's Department badge and a square piece of heavy vellum paper with a crease suggesting he'd folded it to jam it in a pocket. An invitation. Her heart hammered sickeningly as she looked down at it.

Mr. and Mrs. Joseph Collins
Request the honor of your presence
At the marriage of their daughter
Paige Marie
To
Brandon Murphy
Saturday, June 23, at 3:00 p.m.

Lina got stuck on the date. She read it over and over.

Today. He was getting married *today.*

Forget the bachelor party. He'd decided to have a last fling, and *she* had obliged him.

The shower turned off.

Shaking, panicked, desperate, she yanked on her clothes, not bothering to take the time to put on her bra. She had to be gone before he came out of the bathroom. Her car key was still with the money she'd brought in the pocket of her jeans. The realization that he must have paid for her drinks flitted into her head. And why wouldn't he have? It was still cheap sex.

She opened and closed the door as quietly as she could, trying to step lightly on the stairs. At the bottom, she took off at a run, barely pausing to check for traffic before tearing across the road. There were only three cars left in the gravel parking lot: hers, a beaten-up pickup truck and a glossy black Camaro. His, of course, she thought bitterly.

Gasping for breath, Lina unlocked the driver's door of her car and jumped in. She could see the motel in her rearview mirror. The door to their room remained closed. Either he was still in the bathroom, or he was relieved she was gone.

He was likely relieved.

When she pulled onto the road, gravel spit out from beneath her tires.

BRAN SAW THAT the room was empty the instant he opened the bathroom door. His first reaction was shock. Then he swore viciously. How could he be so freaking stupid as to leave his wallet and car keys out here?

Both were still there, at least, his badge beside them. Man, that would have been embarrassing if she'd taken it. Losing his driver's license would be a royal pain, too. He flipped open the wallet, relieved at the sight of not only the driver's license, but also his debit and two credit cards. A little cash was a small price to pay...

But it was there, too. He flipped through the bills, counted. Seemed about right. Had she not even picked up his wallet?

No, of course she hadn't. She wasn't that kind of woman. Of course she wasn't.

Shit, he thought, she did regret the night. The best sex of his life, and she'd run from him, ashamed. And it was his own damn fault. He'd *known* she didn't do things like this, that she was drunk and not thinking straight. What had he expected? That she'd be hanging around, wanting to flirt and talk about when they'd see each other again?

He'd find her...

Yeah, and how was he going to do that? Blonde woman, twenty-five to thirty-five years old, approximately five foot six. The tiny mole he'd seen on her shoulder? Only helpful for identification if she was found dead. For all he knew, she wasn't even from around here. If she was? Alina wasn't a common name…but he had no idea what her last name was, or what she drove. Where she worked, or what she did for a living.

He swore and leaped for the door, but wasn't surprised to discover he was too late. His Camaro sat out in front of the tavern, alone except for a rusting pickup he couldn't in a million years imagine her driving.

While he'd stood here counting bills, she'd made her getaway. Bran groaned and rubbed a hand over his face.

Maybe…she'd find him. If she'd even looked at his badge or opened his wallet, she had one up on him. *She* knew his last name and where he worked.

That was followed by the cold realization that if she didn't come looking, it meant she didn't want to be found, either.

And he had to honor that.

Pocketing the badge and wallet, he glanced down and saw the corner of a piece of paper sticking out from beneath the dresser. The maid could pick it up. Bran dropped a ten-dollar bill on the dresser, then walked out, feeling a couple decades older than he had a few days ago.

CHAPTER TWO

WITH ONLY A week to go until Christmas, Lina Jurick felt exceptionally unfestive. Her parents weren't very happy that she wasn't flying home for the holidays, but pretending to be joyous was beyond her.

It wasn't like she was hiding anything from them. Well, not hiding very much anyway. Once she'd made the decision to carry the baby to term, she'd told them she was pregnant. The only part she'd refused to talk about was the identity of the father. *She* didn't want to think about Bran "short for Brandon" Murphy, who might or might not be married.

After she'd fled, it had occurred to her that he could have gone to the tavern for the same reason she had: he was bummed. Say, because his wedding had been canceled.

That idea was slightly more palatable than the alternative, that she was a last hurrah. But not a whole lot. If his bride-to-be had stood him up right before the wedding, what did that make her, Lina? Some kind of hey-she's-available fill-in?

All cats were gray in the dark, right? And in the morning, when it wasn't dark anymore, he'd had her from behind and never had to look at her face. If he hadn't gotten any sex on what should have been his wedding night, he'd certainly had plenty the night before.

Occasionally she let herself wonder if it had occurred to him he hadn't used a condom that last time. But, really, what difference did it make whether he'd just forgotten or made the decision to wake up the way he liked even though he couldn't protect her? The result was the same.

At least the morning sickness phase was long past. These days, all she had to combat was exhaustion. She needed to go to bed way earlier than normal if she was going to feel anything close to human when her alarm clock went off in the mornings. And, just her luck, middle school kids rode the same buses as high school kids, tying them to a similar schedule. No, worse: her first class was at the obscene hour of seven thirty. High school teachers were able to sleep in ten minutes later.

Today, she should count her blessings. With two weeks off for the holidays, she could sleep as much as she wanted. Catch up on sleep. Store it. If she could think of anything fun to do, she was free for that, too. Wild and crazy? Not a chance. She'd used up her quota the night she got pregnant.

She could take a nap after lunch, then go for a swim later.

A nap and exercise. As a way to spend her first day of vacation, it was such a thriller, even she was depressed. Maybe Maya could get away to have lunch with her.

Maya answered her call, muted the phone for a minute and came back to say, "Yes, please." She lowered her voice. "Mr. Floyd is driving me *nuts*. Must get out of here."

Lina changed from her sweats into maternity jeans and a warm sweater with enough stretch to cover her burgeoning belly and put on boots because they zipped and were less work than bending over to tie laces.

Her mood lifted during the short drive to the bank branch where Maya worked as a loan officer. Once she reached it, she idled briefly out front. Mr. Floyd, the branch manager, discouraged the use of the parking lot for friends and family. If she'd been absolutely determined, she could have squeezed her Kia into a minuscule spot behind a van, but she made a face and decided to skip it. Parking on the cross street made sense anyway; she could pick up a couple of things at the Walgreens on the other corner once she and Maya were back from lunch.

She locked up and walked past the drive-through and the ATM to the front doors, but when she tried to open one, she couldn't. They were locked. What on earth—

Belatedly, she focused on the printed sign plastered to the glass: "Temporarily Closed—Computer Network Issues. We Regret the Inconvenience."

How strange. Maya hadn't said anything, so whatever it was must have just happened. Lina peered in and couldn't see a soul, teller or customer, which wasn't a big shock since this bank had a conference room to the right just inside and restrooms to the left. The only other windows looked in at the currently empty conference room. Past the short hallway, a second set of doors led into the bank proper, and what view she would otherwise have had was partially blocked by one of those standing height desks where you could write a check or fill out a deposit slip before getting in line. From this angle, she could only see one teller window, with no one behind it.

Presumably, IT people were working frantically. Maybe everyone else was gratefully having a cup of coffee, or Mr. Floyd had decided to hold an impromptu staff meeting to be sure nobody was allowed to waste time. Sounded like him.

Still, Maya was entitled to her lunch break. She would surely have called or at least texted to say she was delayed. And, would they really lock the doors instead of letting customers come in for an explanation of the problem?

As Lina backed away from the doors, pondering, she took out her phone. No messages, no texts.

Darn it, people *had* to be inside. Driving past the parking lot, she'd noticed Mr. Floyd's dark gray BMW in its place of honor as well as a couple of other cars. Although those might belong to the IT people rather than customers.

Call Maya, she decided.

But her friend didn't answer her cell phone. Lina didn't leave a message.

Increasingly uneasy, she tried to decide what to do. She could wait in her car for a few minutes and then try again. Go to Walgreens and assume Maya would call when she was ready to leave. But the weirdness of this had her alarmed.

The back door was not only always kept locked, it was also steel and windowless. The only other place she could really see into the bank was the drive-through window, assuming they hadn't pulled down the shade. No cars had gone in or come out since she'd arrived. Why couldn't she use it as a walk-through to bring somebody to talk to her even if only to say, "Yes, we really are closed."

She went back the way she'd come and circled the corner of the building. Feeling almost as though she ought to be tiptoeing, she approached the double drive-through with the center island. Then she saw the explanation for the lack of traffic: a sandwich board blocked the entrance to the drive-through. She presumed the same sign was tacked to the other side.

Not understanding her trepidation, Lina inched up to the window.

The shades hadn't been pulled, but she still couldn't see anyone. Aliens had beamed everyone in the bank up to their spaceship. IT guys had taken employees hostage until they fully understood the hideous mistake someone had made that had frozen up the bank's computers.

Only…shouldn't someone be laboring on one of the computers? Unless the problem was off-site, but if that was so, why wasn't Maya answering her phone and *where was everybody?*

Lina's skin prickled. She shifted a few feet to the left and with a rush of relief saw four people standing in a cluster. Mr. Floyd and Maya and two men. Okay, she'd been silly—except…one of the men held a gun to Maya's temple.

Oh, God, oh, God. This was a bank robbery, happening right in front of her. Without taking her eyes off the scene inside, Lina fumbled for her phone at the bottom of her purse.

The bank manager shook his head. He looked

scared but mulish. At the same time, Maya saw Lina with her face pressed to the glass. Her eyes widened, the terror on her face changing to something else.

The next second, her head blew up.

And then the man who'd shot Lina's best friend turned and saw her.

LEANING BACK IN his desk chair, Bran unwrapped the sandwich he'd just picked up from the deli. He didn't love eating at his desk, but he was trying to cram some work in so he could leave early. He had an appointment to talk to a woman who had been a neighbor of his family when he was a kid. She and her husband had lived right across the street when Bran's little sister, Sheila, was murdered. Apparently Mr. Greaver had died a few years back, but his widow had stayed put. Bran and his brother, Zach, both cops, were trying to get in touch with everyone who'd lived nearby then. Sheila's killer had never been arrested. Despite having no jurisdiction, they intended to accomplish what the investigators at the time had failed to do.

So far, they'd only hit dead ends, but there'd been something in Mrs. Greaver's voice when Bran had talked to her yesterday—

The door behind him burst open.

"Murphy," his lieutenant snapped. "Warring. Where the hell is Warring?"

Bran spun in his desk chair, surprised by the edge in his boss's usually rock-steady voice. "Break room, to get a drink from the machine. What's wrong?"

"Armed robbery at Snoqualmie Community Bank. First responders are on the way. I want you and Warring on it. The caller says she saw a loan officer shot in the head. If they're still in there…"

Bran tossed the sandwich on the desk and jumped to his feet. "How did somebody manage to call out?"

"She didn't. She couldn't understand why the doors were locked midday, so she looked in the drive-through window."

"Where is she now?"

"The Walgreens across the street."

"We're on our way."

He caught Charlie Warring just as he emerged from the break room carrying a can of Pepsi. Seconds later, they jumped into an unmarked sheriff's car and rocketed out of the parking lot, Charlie still groping for the seat belt as he tried to keep from spilling his drink.

"What the hell?"

Bran told him what he knew. During the drive, they both listened to the chatter on the radio. By the time they screeched to a halt outside the bank, they knew that the robbers had been gone when the first deputies arrived. An ambulance rolled up behind them. Two patrol cars with flashing lights were outside.

Charlie and Bran walked in to find the expected chaos. The uniforms had corralled customers and employees in one area, where two women sobbed and everyone else appeared distraught. One of the deputies saw Bran and jerked his head toward the counter that normally separated tellers from customers.

He stopped at a swinging half door. On the other side, two bodies sprawled on the carpeted floor. It wasn't instantly obvious how the man in the suit had been killed, although blood soaked the carpet to one side of him. The woman's body was another story. Blood, brains and bits of bone spattered the wall beyond her. The information had been accurate; no question, somebody had shot her in the head, and from close range.

"Jesus," Charlie murmured. "I bank here. I think she's the loan officer. Pretty."

She wasn't pretty anymore.

Bran pointed to the pile of cell phones, which suggested the robbers had had some foresight. They'd made sure no one texted out or snapped a photo of them.

Another uniform approached. Despite his attempt at stoicism, he appeared shaken. "My partner and I were the first responders. I hope the lady who called this in saw something, because nobody else did. They all agree that two masked men shoved through the doors yelling and waving guns. Customers and tellers were herded behind the counter and made to sit on the floor, facing the far wall—" he nodded in that direction "—and told to clasp their hands on their heads. They could hear what went on, but didn't see anything. I didn't even ask questions, and they started to babble. They tried to be helpful, but they all had different estimates of height, weight, race…" He shook his head. "Don't think you'll get a lot of help there."

"Thanks," Bran said.

Charlie offered to get things started there while Bran went looking for the witness who'd called 911. Charlie Warring was about Bran's age. With any other detective in the department, Bran would have refused, but he and Charlie had developed a trust.

"You suppose the lieutenant has already notified the FBI?" Charlie asked.

"Undoubtedly," Bran said with resignation. He'd never worked with the feds before, but he'd have his chance now. They were all over any bank robbery.

He found the pharmacy doors locked. A man peered at him from a distance away. When Bran held his badge up to the glass, relief appeared on the man's face and he hurried to let him in. With a nod toward the back, he said, "The lady who saw what happened is with the manager. Should I keep the door locked?"

"No need now. The robbers are long gone. But locking up was smart."

Bran took a moment to determine that no customers had been present when the witness came tearing in. Then he strode down an aisle and, at the back of the store, found an unlocked door marked "Employees Only." Past a restroom and what appeared to be a break room was an office. He knocked and identified himself as police.

A woman called, "Come in."

There were two women inside, one with her back to him, the other behind the desk. She rose to her feet at the sight of him. From the nice suit, he guessed she was the store manager. "I'm Laverne Dailey," she said.

"Detective Bran Murphy."

"Are the robbers still in the bank?" she asked.

"No, they were gone by the time the first unit arrived. I can assure you we'll do everything in our power to identify and arrest them." He heard the coldness in his voice.

The sight of those bodies had hit him harder than usual, maybe because of the location and the identity of the victims. This wasn't a domestic, or the fallout from a bar brawl. The dead weren't drug dealers or gang members. The bank was the kind of business where people expected to be safe. To the best of his knowledge, there'd never been a bank robbery in this county. And bank robbers didn't usually kill.

"A uniformed officer will be stopping by to ask some questions, just in case an employee noticed activity by the bank."

During his speech, the woman sitting with her back to him hadn't turned around. In fact, she hadn't given any sign she'd even noticed his arrival. She hunched over, her arms crossed as if she was hugging herself. Traumatized, and why wouldn't she be?

Honey-colored hair was bundled on the back of her head. His gaze fastened on it. Some people's hair was all one color. Hers had threads of pale gold, brown and red amongst the predominant dark blonde. He bet if he studied it long enough, he'd identify a dozen or more colors that together added up to a gorgeous, heavy mass of hair that… he knew.

No. It couldn't be.

He grabbed the second chair in front of the desk, pulled it to face hers and sat down. "Miss—"

She looked up and his mouth went dry. The woman who had haunted his dreams for months looked at him with red-rimmed, puffy eyes.

"You," she said flatly.

So she had recognized his voice. Bran let his gaze move over her, and what he saw made his heart stop beating.

She was pregnant. The curve of her belly was unmistakable. Bran wasn't an expert on pregnancy, but she had to be past the first three months or so, when women didn't much show. She wasn't swollen so big he'd worry about her going into labor right now, either. If he had to guess—

Jesus. If he had to guess, he'd put her at five or six months.

Six months ago, almost to the day, he'd made love to her without using a condom. He'd worried about that for a long time, even as remembering what it felt like to have her without the irritating barrier of latex heated his blood.

When he lifted his stunned gaze to her face, he found wariness had joined the grief and myriad of other emotions already there. Bran opened his mouth but had just enough self-control to close it before he said the obvious. *Did you plan to tell me?* Later, when they were alone, he'd be asking that question. Right now, he had a job to do. And she'd seen something horrific enough, he wasn't about to kick her when she was down.

"Ms. Dailey, may we borrow your office or the break room?"

The manager understood what he was asking. "Please, stay here," she said, coming around the desk. "Lina, are you sure I can't get you a drink?"

"That's a good idea," Bran said. "Something with sugar. She's in shock."

"I don't need—" Lina's brief defiance collapsed. "Thank you. But no caffeine, please."

Laverne Dailey squeezed her shoulder. "Of course not."

Lina and Bran sat in silence until the manager returned with a 7Up. Bran cracked it open and handed it to Lina. "Drink. The sugar will steady you."

After a moment, she nodded. The door closed quietly behind Ms. Dailey.

Lina took a swallow, but her hand was shaking, so he took the can from her and set it on the desk. "I need your full name," he said, wincing at how stiffly that came out.

He read the desperation in her eyes. "I wasn't imagining things, was I? Maya is dead."

"I'm afraid so. Maya…?"

"Lee. She is…she was a loan officer. And my best friend," she whispered, desolate.

Battling the need to draw her into his arms, he said, "I'm sorry for your loss, and that you had to see something so terrible."

She sucked in a breath. "Jurick." She spelled it. "That's my last name. I'm Alina Jurick."

"You live locally, I take it." He couldn't help the wryness in his tone.

Her eyes slid away before meeting his again. "Yes. I live in Clear Creek and teach at the middle school."

"What do you teach, Lina?"

"Social studies."

Bran only vaguely recalled his long-ago middle school classes. Social studies had been a mishmash of history and government, maybe a little anthropology and archaeology thrown in. He'd have liked to ask more, like why she had chosen to work with kids that age, but made himself stay on topic.

"Okay. You came to do some banking."

She shook her head. "No, Maya and I were going to have lunch. I talked to her about fifteen minutes before I arrived. I parked on the street instead of in the lot, because her boss doesn't even let employees park there, never mind friends."

He heard about her perplexity when she found the doors locked in the middle of the day, and resisted asking why the hell she hadn't called the cops right then.

"It was the sign," she said.

"Sign?"

"It was taped to one of the doors." She told him what it said.

"It's not there anymore. Which means they grabbed it on the way out."

"I think there was another one at the head of the drive-through. If they were in a hurry, they might have left that one."

"Good," he said. "Give me a second."

Charlie answered immediately and promised to send someone out to check.

Bran returned his phone to his belt.

"It did seem strange," Lina said. "But...normal strange. You know what I mean? I sort of knew something was wrong. But, um, there's this feeling of unreality. Who expects something like..." She wobbled to a stop, then clapped her hand over her mouth.

Bran lunged out of his chair and grabbed the wastebasket, putting it in front of her. She bent over and retched. When she seemed done, he found tissues on a credenza and gave her a handful, then urged her to sip more of the soda. At some point in there, he'd come to be crouched beside her, rubbing her back.

The look she gave him held such misery, he said, "Oh, hell, Lina," and rose, pulling her to her feet and into his arms. For a moment she stood stiff. He was about to release her when she made a muffled sound, leaned on him and seemed to go boneless. They stood like that for a long time. Inhaling her scent, he cradled the back of her head with one hand while he held her up with his other arm.

The hard mound of her belly felt odd wedged between them. It was like a purse or a—no, not a basketball—a soccer ball. Maybe one of those kid-size ones. Then he had the dazed thought that what he felt between them wasn't kid-size— it *was* a kid. A whole, complete person in the making.

That this particular baby might be his was something he couldn't let himself think about, not yet.

Once he would have sworn her belly quivered, but probably all of her had.

Finally, she sighed and didn't so much ease back as collapse onto the chair. "I'm sorry. You must have more important things to do than wait while I freak out. I guess you need to hear what I saw, don't you?"

"I do, but you don't have anything to be sorry for. Anybody would have been shaken up."

He didn't recall ever being reluctant to push a witness to tell her story like this before. Bran hoped he was a compassionate man, but softer emotions weren't in his repertoire.

"I couldn't see anyone else. There had to be tellers in there."

She didn't want to ask whether they were dead, too, he guessed.

Bran resumed his seat. "Two tellers, two customers. The robbers made them sit on the floor behind the counter, hands on their heads, facing away from the confrontation you saw. They're shaken up, but not hurt."

She gave a jerky nod, then continued, telling him she hadn't really looked at one of the two men, but she knew he'd worn a ski mask. "So I couldn't have seen his face anyway. I think he was shorter than the other robber. Mr. Floyd— that's the bank manager—isn't tall. Like five foot eight? They were about the same height. He was thin. He had a gun, too."

This *he*, Bran supposed, was bank robber number two, not Mr. Floyd. "Was he facing you?"

"No, he was mostly turned away. I think he was threatening Mr. Floyd, who was refusing to do something." Her beautiful eyes widened. "Mr. Floyd...was he hurt?"

"I don't have identities yet, but a man was killed as well as your friend."

"Oh, no," she whispered. Her knuckles showed white as she wrung her hands.

"I'm sorry," he said again, feeling helpless. "Saying no to armed men threatening him wasn't very smart."

"No." Lina was quiet for a minute. "Maya didn't like him. I don't think any of the employees did. He was really full of himself, and sanctimonious. You know? It would be just like him to think he could stand up to those men because he was important and principled and of course they'd back down."

In other words, the guy was both a prick and an idiot.

He watched Lina collect herself. "The other one, he had the barrel of his gun pressed to Maya's temple. She looked so scared." She swallowed. "Maya saw me."

"What?"

"I think she kind of jerked and—" Lina did some deep breathing "—he shot her. Her head just…"

Bran covered her writhing hands with one of his. "Try to step back, as if it was a movie and not real. Did the guy pull the trigger because he was startled? Or do you think he'd been ordered to kill her?"

She stared at him, but he could tell she was replaying what she'd seen. "I think Mr. Floyd had been told that if he didn't cooperate, they'd kill Maya. And he wouldn't, so they did."

"That's what I think, too," Bran said gently. "Her seeing you had nothing to do with her death."

"Yes, but—" She gulped. "He shot her and then he turned. He saw *me*."

Bran's blood ran cold.

She shuddered. "And...and I saw *him*."

"He wasn't wearing a mask?"

She shook her head. "Why would he let anyone see his face?" she begged.

He didn't know. They must have known law enforcement would be watching the robbery within half an hour. Banks all had cameras.

"He couldn't shoot you through the teller's window," Bran said slowly. "They're bullet-proof."

"I don't know if he even came to the window. I ducked, really fast. And then I ran straight across the drive-through lanes and the side street instead of going to my car or...or to the alley to try to hide. In case he burst out the front or back door."

"That was smart." He fought to hide the rage and fear that made it hard to breathe. "Lina, did you recognize him?"

She shook her head, but some crinkles formed on her forehead. "Not really, although...he looked sort of familiar. Do you know what I mean?" she appealed to him. "He might just have had an ordinary face, but it's like, oh, if you see someone out of context and can't place them. They're a stranger, but not."

"Like a grocery checker you notice at the next table when you're eating out."

"Exactly like that," she said gratefully. "But it was such a quick glimpse..."

"If his face doesn't show up clearly on video,

we'll have you sit down with a police artist. However briefly you saw the man, I'm betting the artist and you can come up with a portrait."

She looked doubtful, but said, "I'll try."

"What worries me is that he saw *you*, Lina. You're memorable, not ordinary."

"I'm not."

"Yeah, you are. I had no trouble recognizing you." If he sounded a little dry, who could blame him?

"Yes, but you and I—" Color rose in her cheeks. "We…"

He knew what they'd done.

"I mean, we spent quite a while together. Talking and…"

Yep. *And.* They'd done a lot of that, too.

Blushing furiously, she said, "The other people in there must have seen *something*. And…and they'd have heard what was said."

"If we get anything useful from those who were in the bank, I'll worry less about you. From what I heard before I came over here, I'm not optimistic. It's also possible he'd just pulled the mask off when you saw him."

She stared at him, stricken. "If he did…that means he was going to kill Maya either way, doesn't it?"

"I'm afraid so" was the best he could do. The video could be grainy; the guy's face might be caught at an angle so that distinguishing features weren't clear. Or no camera had pointed the right way to capture his image at the moment he'd been unmasked. But her friend had had a close look at him.

"Oh, God." She hugged herself again.

Very aware of the passing minutes, Bran said, "Lina, I have to get back to the bank. You and I need to talk, but we'll save that for later. I'm only going to ask one thing right now. Is that baby you're carrying mine?"

She seemed to shrink into herself, making him feel like a bastard, but he had to know. After a minute, her head bobbed. "Yes."

Damn. It was like seeing someone running out in front of his car, knowing he would never be able to brake in time. His vision had sharpened and time slowed, but his reactions had slowed, too.

He could only nod. "All right." Really? It was all hunky-dory? *No problemo?*

Do your job. "Lina, I won't be able to get away for hours. I don't want you to go home until we know more, in case the guy did recognize you. Do you have family close by? Or a friend who will let you spend the night if necessary?"

She stared at him. "But… I don't have anything with me. Except my purse." Looking more like a satchel, it sat by her feet.

"As soon as I break free, I'll come get you. Then we'll figure out what to do. But if you're the only one who saw his face and this guy by any chance did know you, he can't afford to let you identify him. Do you understand?"

She nodded, her face so white he was afraid she might keel over. But her back stayed rigid. "Yes. I saw what he's willing to do."

Damn. She had.

"Tell me where you'll be."

"Let me make a call." She dug in the bag for her phone, and a moment later was talking to someone. She finished by saying, "I'll tell you all about it when I get there. Thank you, Isabel." The call ended. She told him the friend's name and address.

He took her phone from her and added his number to her contacts, then put hers in his phone. "I'll walk you to your car."

They both thanked the manager on the way out. As they crossed the street, Bran said, "I'm going to have you take a look at the parking lot. Do you remember what vehicles were here when you arrived?"

"Yes." They walked past the bank so she could see the lot. "Those are the same cars that were here then."

"Okay. Where did your friend park?"

"I noticed it on Maple." That was the street

they'd just crossed. My car is only half a block from hers."

"Is that why you parked where you did?"

"No, there wasn't any room in front of the bank." She saw something on his face. "They didn't park in the lot, did they?"

"No, they'd have gotten as close to the front door as they could. Preferably blocking any view of the bank from passing traffic."

"Close to the front...there was a gold Camry. I noticed it because my parents have one like it. And a cargo van. My car is really small, so I could have squeezed in between the van and the Camry, but I'm not very good at parallel parking and it would have been tight."

"Okay," he said, keeping his tone relaxed. He didn't want her to freeze up. "Describe the van to me."

"It was white, with panels instead of windows along the side. On the back, too, I'm pretty sure. I remember thinking I wouldn't like having to rely totally on mirrors."

"Was there a company name on the side or the door? A decal of any kind? A bumper sticker?"

But she was shaking her head. "Nothing. I doubt I'd have noticed a bumper sticker. I mean, I barely glanced at the back of the van when I was thinking of trying to squeeze in behind it."

"I don't suppose you noticed the license plate."

"Not a chance." She hesitated. "I guess it might have caught my eye if it had been an out-of-state license or a custom one."

That was his guess, too, given how extraordinarily observant she had proved herself to be.

With a hand on her arm, he nudged her into movement again. "Getting away was the smart thing for you to do. You had no reason to focus on the van."

Cops clustered outside the bank's front door. The medical examiner was just going in. Bran nodded at him.

"Which car is yours?" he asked Lina, looking to the cross street.

"The Kia."

He had her point out her friend's, too, before asking, "You feel steady enough to drive?"

She took a deep breath. "Yes. Anyway, it's not that far to Isabel's."

He insisted on walking her to her peanut of a car and watched as she wedged herself behind the wheel and adjusted and fastened the seat belt. How in hell did women who were eight months pregnant still reach the pedals?

Shaking the thought off, he waited until she had closed the door and then rolled down the window to look up at him.

"Okay," he said. "Keep an eye out behind you on the way. If any other vehicle seems to be sticking with you, I want you to come right back here. Call me, too. Don't wait until you get here. Do you understand?"

Lina bit her lip but nodded.

"And call if you remember anything else you think I should know."

"I will."

"If it looks like I won't make it before bedtime, I'll let you know. This Isabel understands you might have to stay, right?"

"Yes. She teaches at the middle school, too. We've gotten to be good friends."

One hand flat on the roof of her car, Bran looked down at her. "I'd suggest you have a glass of wine, but I guess you can't do that."

She actually tried to smile. "Probably one glass wouldn't hurt anything, but I made a no-alcohol, no-caffeine vow once I realized I was pregnant."

"You don't smoke, do you?"

"No. I never have. And I wouldn't."

Feeling foolish, he nodded. "I'll call, Lina."

Without another word, she pushed a button so her window glided up and put on her turn signal before pulling out onto the street. Afraid she'd get a ticket if she didn't? No, he thought; Lina Jurick was a law-abiding citizen. A good girl, who had done something very uncharacteristic the night she'd gone to a cheap motel with him.

Standing where he was for longer than he

should have, watching until the little Kia turned out of sight three blocks away, he wondered if his promise to call had sounded reassuring to her, or whether she'd taken it as a threat.

He swore under his breath. Would she ever have told him about the baby if they hadn't come face-to-face? Part of him was scared shitless. And part of him…he didn't know…and couldn't take the time to untangle it all.

Bran turned and walked into the bank.

CHAPTER THREE

WAITING WAS REALLY HARD.

After one look at Lina when she first arrived at the Moreno's house, Isabel sent her two kids to their bedrooms. Then she sat Lina down in the kitchen and insisted she nibble on soda crackers and drink ginger ale while she told the whole, awful story.

Well, she didn't mention that, to complete the trauma, she had just come face-to-face with the father of her baby. Who happened to be the investigator.

Not even Maya had known who the father was. All Lina would ever say was that it had been a mistake. Admitting that she'd gotten drunk and willingly had repeated sex with a complete stranger in a cheap motel room? No.

Steadier, Lina was able to have a bowl of soup and half a sandwich with Isabel and both kids, who were told only that Lina was waiting for a friend to call. At three and five, they nodded incuriously and chattered away. Predictably, they were excited about Christmas. Their tree was up in the living room, but without gifts under it.

"Carmen might be able to keep her hands off them," Isabel said, once the children had trotted off to the living room to watch a Disney movie on DVD, "but Ricky never could. They've both been hyper from the minute I left work Tuesday."

Of course, the women's conversation reverted quickly to the horrific scene at the bank. Isabel had met Maya through Lina and had to deal with her own shock.

"In Clear Creek!" she kept exclaiming.

Lina felt the same. She read in the newspaper about things like this happening, but it never did in this small, rural county. Except now she wondered if she hadn't been naive. Crimes of some kind must occupy Bran and all those other cops she'd seen swarming the bank.

Eventually she wound down as if her battery was failing. She had to ask if there was someplace she could nap. She was afraid she'd have had to lay her cheek on the table and sleep right there otherwise.

Once alone, exhaustion claimed her before she could shatter. It was as if her body had to shut down.

Hours later, she woke up disoriented. Night had somehow fallen. She'd have been completely in the dark if not for a night-light glowing softly on the dresser.

She was in Carmen's room, Lina remembered. Posters, wallpaper border and curtains all featured horses. Five-year-old Carmen had told her earnestly that she wanted to grow up to be a horsie rancher and a ballerina. She was dainty enough to be a ballerina, but admitted to having been on a pony only twice. Mama and Papa— she had looked daggers at her mother—wouldn't buy her a horse.

Lina stumbled to the bathroom across the hall where she washed her face and brushed and braided her hair. For a minute, she stared unseeingly into the mirror.

Oh, dear God. Maya. She wanted it to have been a nightmare, but knew better.

From the smells, Isabel must be cooking. Lina felt queasy, as if the morning sickness had reappeared.

Isabel looked her over anxiously when she appeared in the kitchen. "You look better. Would you like a pop? Or juice?"

That might help. Lina poured herself a glass of cranberry juice and sat down. "I'm being useless. I'm sorry."

"No, no. I wouldn't have let you help," her friend said. She nodded toward the bag Lina had plopped at her feet. "You should call the detective. He called *me* because you weren't answering. I think you scared him."

"I didn't hear it ring." Lina checked her phone. He'd tried her four times and left two messages. Listening to them, she realized Isabel was right; he did sound worried.

He answered on the first ring.

"I'm sorry," she said before he could say anything but her name. "I took a nap. I must have really conked out."

"So Isabel said. She checked on you for me."

"She did?"

"I'm winding things up here. Why don't I come over? I can update you on what we've learned, and then I think you can safely go home."

"Oh, thank goodness! Does that mean the camera was pointing at him?"

"Not exactly. I'll explain when I get there."

Either somebody was within earshot or he was determined to sit down face-to-face with her.

Or it wasn't really the bank robbery and Maya he wanted to talk about. He wouldn't confront her about the pregnancy here, with Isabel and maybe Eduardo or the kids within earshot, would he?

If not, he'd want to follow her home. There'd be no escaping the conversation she dreaded.

The one we have to have, she reminded herself. She'd always known she would have to tell him about the baby and give him the chance to be involved in her life. She just...kept putting it off.

"Okay," she said. "I'll wait until you get here."

"Ten minutes," he promised, and was gone.

He hadn't asked for directions, but she supposed he could find any place, even if it was within the city limits and therefore not in his jurisdiction, which was unincorporated county.

Predictably, Isabel insisted they should at least stay for dinner. She'd made plenty. Lina thanked her, but said, "Detective Murphy is a police officer. He feels obligated to tell me some of what they've learned, but after that he'd probably like to just get home."

"But it will be ready—" Isabel laughed and shook her head. "I have this ridiculous need to feed people. I'm turning into my mother. Ignore me."

Laughing for the first time in many hours, Lina hugged her petite, dark-haired friend. "If you're turning into your mother, it can't be such a bad thing. And if you mean it about dinner, I'll ask Bran—I mean, Detective Murphy—when he gets here."

Isabel's eyes sharpened at Lina's slip, but she didn't comment on it. "Either way is fine."

Bran had been more than kind today, but the closest thing to real emotion she'd seen on his face was the shock when he recognized her...

and saw that she was pregnant. Otherwise, he'd been guarded, even remote. She couldn't imagine him wanting to sit down with a cheerful family to share their dinner.

When the doorbell rang, she let him in, feeling an immediate punch of awareness. He wouldn't have to say a word or do anything to dominate any gathering. He did that with just his physical presence and those piercing blue eyes that took in everything.

"Why don't you come in and meet my friend?" Lina suggested.

"Sure." He took one step in and inhaled. "God, that smells good. I'm starved. No lunch."

"We're invited to stay for dinner. Eduardo should be home any minute. They have two kids, though…"

His stomach chose that moment to rumble, and one side of his mouth tipped up. "Do you think there's really enough to go around?"

"I'm sure."

She'd barely introduced him to Isabel when they heard the garage door rising. Lina didn't know Isabel's husband well, but had liked what she'd seen of him. He was a strong, stocky man not that much taller than her, his skin much darker than his wife's. His kids raced to greet him, and he had a huge smile as he tossed each one into the air in turn before gently setting them down.

Then he looked at Lina. "Isabel called to tell me. What a terrible thing to happen, and for you to see it…"

"I appreciate Isabel taking me in. And—" she smiled at the little girl "—Carmen letting me borrow her bed for a nap."

She had started to introduce the two men when it became apparent they already knew each other.

The next thing she knew they were all seated around the dining room table eating chile verde con puerco with refried beans and warm corn tortillas. Lina guessed Isabel had been cooking all afternoon, but maybe it was one way she enjoyed using her days off. Lina barely nibbled at her dinner, hoping no one noticed, but Bran ate enough for both of them.

He answered a few questions from the adults about the robbery, careful not to say anything the kids shouldn't hear, then began talking to Eduardo about his business, Clear Creek Power Equipment. It sounded as if he had rented equipment from him a few times. He had also investigated a burglary from the business.

Isabel taught biology and coached the girls' soccer team. "They asked me to take over the basketball team, too," she joked, "but I had to admit it isn't my sport." They all laughed at that. Isabel might have been five foot one. Her husband teased her, saying she could make a basket if she were standing on his shoulders.

After accepting hugs and promising to call, Lina and Bran left.

"I'll follow you home," he said, his tone completely inflexible.

Shivering, Lina didn't argue. Snow had been forecast for the next day or two, and she wondered if it might start falling tonight. They could hardly stand out here on the sidewalk and talk.

Bran's black Camaro hugged her bumper all the way home. At her complex, he parked illegally but stuck something on his dashboard that she assumed said Police or the like, and followed her into the lobby where she collected her mail before leading him to the elevator.

As it rose, he said, "Your friends are nice people."

"They are. You already knew Eduardo."

"Because of the investigation."

The elevator doors opened and they went down the hall to her apartment. "And you rented equipment to work on your house," she said, curious about him.

"I live in an apartment, too. I've been helping my brother work on an old place he's restoring. I'd have said it was a dump, but it's starting to look good."

She unlocked the door. "You're lucky to have family nearby."

"He only moved here this spring. We'd…lost touch."

Lina wondered about the hesitation, but only nodded. Once inside her apartment, she watched as he assessed it, starting with the small, decorated tree that sat on a tabletop, then taking in her bookcases, furniture, the opening into the kitchen.

"Can I get you a cup of coffee?" she asked, as much to fill the silence as anything.

He shook his head. "Not when you won't be having any."

"It's no trouble…"

"Thank you, Lina, but no." He nodded toward her sofa. "Why don't you sit down?"

She did, her apprehension making her feel like a child who knew she was in trouble. So much for having the upper hand because this was *her* territory.

"What did you mean by *not exactly*? Did you or didn't you see his face?"

Bran sat in a maple rocking chair facing her across the coffee table. "There's not a good view."

"How can that be?"

He sighed. "Cameras are aimed in front of the tellers, not behind them. One placed to the side let us see your friend and the manager with the two men, but it wasn't a good angle. Both men wore knit ski masks. They stormed in, brandished weapons and yelled to intimidate the employees and the two customers who were in the bank at that point. Only one teller was at work, and she froze and didn't push the alarm. They took away everyone's cell phones. As I said, they were made to sit on the floor with their backs turned. According to one of the women, they were told that the first person trying to sneak a look would be shot."

"So none of them did."

"No. They were scared out of their skulls. None of them could even describe body types. They all agreed both men were big, which is typical when witnesses are scared. They did confirm that you were right about what was going on. The manager was refusing to open the vault. The robber who did the talking said they'd kill the woman if he didn't do what they wanted. He said no again."

A whimper escaped her.

He half stood, then sat again, his hands gripping the arms of the chair. "I'm sorry, Lina."

She took some deep breaths and was finally able to nod.

"When the guy grabbed your friend, she fought. From what we can see on the video, it looks like she hooked her fingernails in the knit mask and pulled it sideways. He wouldn't have been able to see at all. Subduing her, he couldn't fiddle with it to align the eyeholes, so he wrenched it off. After he shot her, he grabbed it and put it back on. He wasn't without it for more than a minute, if that."

"But Mr. Floyd would have seen him, too."

"Yeah. That was a death sentence for him, I'm afraid. That and—"

She could tell he didn't want to finish the thought. So she did. "And trying to stand up to them?"

"I'd have put it a little differently," Bran said. "If he'd cooperated from the beginning…"

Maya and he would both be alive. Lina swallowed and nodded.

"We'll definitely want you to sit down with the artist," he continued. "A couple of FBI agents arrived, and they're pretty excited that you saw him. It turns out they've been after these two for a while."

"What do you mean? Have they robbed other banks?"

"This is at least the third, and there's a possibility of others. These guys have used the signs before. They took them away when they left after the two previous robberies, but witnesses had noticed them and remembered the wording, which was identical to what you saw and to the one taped to that sandwich board. You were right— they did take down the one on the door as they fled, but left the one at the drive-through. Unfortunately, neither have any fingerprints. These guys are careful."

Hung up on what he'd said at the beginning of that last speech, she asked, "What do you mean, a possibility of others?"

"There've been a couple others in the past eighteen months that were so similar, it's likely the same two guys. Ski masks, yelling, making everyone sit behind the counter with their backs turned. No one saw signs."

"If no one happened to come to the door or try to go through the drive-through..."

"Exactly," he said.

"I remember the news mentioning several bank robberies not that long ago," she said, trying to recall details. "But weren't they down south?"

"The two where we know they used the signs were both in Pierce County. One in Tacoma, one in Lakewood." Two hours away, then. "The others that may be linked happened in Issaquah and Monroe."

So, midway. Both were at least an hour drive from Clear Creek.

"Because of the string of robberies, we're assuming the two men are not locals," Bran said. "The agent in charge of the investigation suspects that they live in Pierce County, but decided it was getting too hot down there for them to risk hitting another bank in the area. Some had taken additional precautions, including armed guards, and these two were smart to be nervous."

"That's why you think I don't have to worry." She felt lighter, suddenly.

"It's likely that the guy just had one of those faces that isn't especially distinctive."

"Have they killed anyone before?"

He shook his head.

Lina absorbed the information. So much anger rose in her, for that instant she was almost glad Mr. Floyd was dead, too. If not for him, Maya wouldn't have died. He'd put the bank's money ahead of her life.

They sat in silence for long enough, she had trouble making herself look at Bran. Could he tell what she was thinking? If she didn't say anything else, would he go away?

If he did, that would only give her longer to tie herself up in knots. *Ask. You have to ask.*

She took a deep breath. "Are you married?"

He jerked, rocking the chair. "What? Why would you think—" Then he fell silent.

"I saw the invitation. You left it on the dresser. It was…it was your wedding day."

"Oh, hell." He sounded weary. "That's why you took off, isn't it?"

"Yes."

"I'm not married, Lina. I wouldn't have slept

with you the night before my wedding, for Christ's sake. How could you think—"

"I didn't know you. I still don't know you." With an effort, she calmed herself. "But you were planning to get married."

"We'd called it off a couple days before I met you." He made an odd sound. "She called it off."

"It's not very flattering to me, either way," Lina said. "All I knew was that I'd been stupid." So much for calm. Every tumultuous emotion she'd felt today coalesced into a burst of rage. "You didn't use a condom!"

"No." Honesty and regret showed stark on his hard face. "I didn't even think about it until later. I'm sorrier than I can say. I...worried." He paused. "I tried to find you."

Because he was afraid he'd gotten her pregnant, not because he wanted to see her again. Good to know.

"If you saw the invitation, you knew my name."

She bent her head and focused on her hands, clenched into fists on her thighs. "Yes."

"Were you ever going to tell me?" For the first time, anger crackled in his voice, too.

"Yes." She made herself lift her head and meet those blue eyes. "I swear I was."

"When?"

"Soon." She'd been telling herself the same

thing for months. *Soon*. More honestly, Lina said, "Before she's born."

He looked stunned. "She?"

"Yes. I had an ultrasound. I'm having a girl."

"You mean, *we're* having a girl."

She didn't blame him for the renewed anger, even though she had good reason to be mad, too. "It's *we* if, well, you believe this is your baby. And you plan to take responsibility."

"Yeah," he said hoarsely. "I believe you. And of course I do. This is my fault."

"This?" She shot to her feet. "If you see this baby as some horrible mistake you feel duty-bound to take responsibility for, forget it!"

Instead of fighting back, he let out a pained sound and rubbed both hands over his face. "Lina, will you sit down?"

She wanted to tell him this was *her* baby and he could take a hike. But she suspected her volatile emotions had more to do with hormones and the horror of the day than with anything he'd said. Slowly, she lowered herself again to the sofa.

He sounded inexpressibly weary when he said, "You've had time to come to terms with it. I haven't."

"You're right," she said stiffly. "I'm sorry."

"Did you consider an abortion?"

She closed her eyes and made herself be honest. "Briefly. I was…pretty freaked out. But, you

know, I'm thirty-two. I want to have children. I
can be a good mother on my own."

"You won't be on your own."

She couldn't deny that financial support would
be welcome. A teacher's salary wasn't fabulous.
Even if she could work up until the birth, she
would miss the last three months of the school
year, which would eat up a fair amount of her
savings.

"Do you have other children?" she blurted.
Why hadn't she wondered before?

"No. God, no. I've never been married." A
muscle twitched in his jaw. "You?"

"I'm divorced."

At her answer, emotion crossed his face. She
couldn't quite decipher it.

At last he nodded. "There's more we'll have to
talk about, but right now I just want to say one
thing. From here on out, this baby ties us together.
It would help if you could trust me."

He hadn't gotten mad. He almost sounded…
gentle. Lina took some deep breaths and remembered the hope she'd felt that morning six months
ago, before she saw the wedding invitation. What
had he done that was really so awful? Face it,
she'd readily agreed to spend the night with him.
He had gone so far as to give her an out when he
asked if she'd be sorry in the morning, and she

knew in her heart he wouldn't have taken her to bed if she'd said yes, or even maybe.

Not using a condom had been unbelievably stupid, of course, but he'd probably been hungover.

She was making excuses for him.

Well, who was she to talk? The responsibility had been shared. Drowsy or not, *she* should have thought about a condom, too.

And…he was right. He would forever be her child's father.

"I…I think I can," she said shakily. "Trust you, I mean."

"Thank you." Instead of leaving, he asked, "Do you feel all right? You're not having any problems?"

"So far, no big problems. I was sick to my stomach for a couple months, but mostly right now I just need more sleep than usual."

He gazed at her, unblinking. "What do you mean, *so far*? And do you have problems that aren't *big*?"

"Nothing ominous." Although she worried constantly. "My blood pressure is a little higher than the doctor would like. She's leaning on me to get plenty of exercise, which I'm doing. Otherwise… things can go wrong later in the pregnancy, but that's rare. I've always been healthy. My mother had no difficulties in childbirth." When he failed to look convinced, she added, "It is all natural, you know."

"Do you feel the baby moving?"

She smiled and looked down to see that she had laid an open hand on her swollen belly. "Yes. It's amazing. The first time—" she lifted her head "—it was a flutter, like a butterfly inside me. But she's already getting stronger. She'll be kicking me before I know it."

He appeared unwillingly fascinated. "I've never really been around many pregnant women. Today I wondered how you'll manage to drive when you get further along."

She made a face. "I don't know. I want to work as long as I can, though, which means driving."

"At least you'll have the summer."

"Combined with maternity leave, it'll give me nearly six months off, thank God. I have a bad feeling that leaving her in day care will be hard."

Lina would swear he was making calculations, but he didn't share them with her. Instead he shook his head after a minute. "Man."

"I'll bet you wish you hadn't gotten out of bed this morning."

"But you were going to surprise me with the news one of these days anyway, weren't you?"

Lina didn't like the sardonic note in his voice. He didn't believe she would have told him. She'd have liked to be offended, but couldn't really blame him. After all, she'd procrastinated for months.

"I would have."

He rose abruptly and said, "I'll let you know when we get the sketch artist scheduled. The holiday may complicate that. I assume you're off work."

"We go back the fourth."

"Can you make yourself available tomorrow for the FBI agents to interview you?"

"Yes."

His gaze settled on her Christmas tree before returning to her. "Are you expecting family?"

She wasn't expecting anyone. Did she have to tell him the truth? He'd think she was pathetic.

"My family lives near Minneapolis. Flying didn't sound like fun right now—" she touched her stomach "—so I decided not to join them."

He frowned a little. "Won't you be celebrating with friends?"

"Maya—" Her voice hitched. "Maya was my best friend."

"I'm sorry I reminded you."

"Did you think I'd forget?" she asked incredulously.

"No." A man she suspected was rarely hesitant, Bran lingered, looking down at her. "You're likely to have nightmares, Lina."

"I didn't this afternoon when I napped."

"It'll all catch up with you." On that cheerful note, he nodded. "I'll call in the morning. Lock up after me."

She followed him to the door. He hovered momentarily just outside as if he wanted to say something else, but finally dipped his head again and walked away without looking back.

Lina closed the door and locked it, then sagged against it, the painted steel cool beneath her forehead. Thoughts and images tumbled in her head like clothes in the dryer.

Maya staring at her. Her head... The monster seeing her. Tearing across the street, expecting a bullet to strike her any moment.

And then the shock of having Bran walk in.

At least she'd gotten the dreaded meeting over with, but...

From here on out, we're tied together.

Lina moaned and bumped her head repeatedly against the door.

CHAPTER FOUR

BRAN SHOULD HAVE gone straight home, but his car seemed to steer itself across town to his brother's house. Christmas lights glittered like icicles around the eaves, and a warm glow from the windows told him Zach and Tess were still up. He glanced at his watch: 7:34. Of course they hadn't gone to bed. Bran realized how unbalanced he felt. With a snort, he thought, *Unbalanced? How about stupefied?* His damn head was spinning. The day felt as if it had already lasted twenty-four hours at least.

He turned off the engine but hesitated. He should have called first. And…was he really ready to tell anyone else?

Bran guessed he must be, or he wouldn't be here.

With a sigh, he got out and crossed the lawn, bounding up the steps to the porch. He rang the bell and waited. No surprise, Zach had put in a new front door with a peephole. He worried about Tess, and for good reason. After the two of them witnessed an ugly crime committed by another sheriff's deputy, she had been terrorized. Even though Andrew Hayes, the deputy, had been convicted of attempted first degree murder for trying to kill Tess, Zach hadn't let down his guard. Bran didn't blame him.

Zach opened the door. If he was surprised, it didn't show. There was still tension between the two of them—reconnecting after twenty-five years wasn't easy—but tonight Bran saw only welcome.

"Hey, come in. I hear you had an exciting day."

He didn't know the half of it.

"It was a little out of the ordinary," Bran agreed. "I was heading home, but somehow I ended up here."

"Have you eaten? We have leftovers."

"Thanks, but I had a good dinner. I'd sent Lina—uh, our principal witness—to a friend's house, and when I went to get her, they fed us. Best Mexican food I've eaten in years, if ever."

A slightly raised eyebrow told him he hadn't distracted Zach from his slip. But it didn't matter—wasn't he here to spill his guts?

"Bran!" Tess had popped out of the kitchen and, smiling, came toward the two men. She rose on tiptoe and kissed him on the cheek, something she'd taken to doing lately. No, not lately—since her wedding day. She'd apparently decided Bran was her brother-in-law, so by God she'd treat him like family whether he liked it or not.

The odd thing was, he did like it, even if he hadn't said so. He liked Tess. She was a gutsy woman. He liked that she was making his brother happy. Their screwed up childhoods had left Zach determined never to marry or have a family, a resolve that crashed and burned when he couldn't run from Tess. Keeping her safe had meant keeping her close.

"If this is a bad time…"

She frowned. "Don't be silly. Do you want a beer?"

"Uh…thanks. Sure."

"Zach?"

"Yeah, I'll take one, too."

They got comfortable in the living room, which was one of the first rooms they had finished remodeling. The day Bran came to help replace the roof, the wood floors in the whole house were worn, and there had been holes in the walls in here. Zach had applied a thin coat of plaster over the new wallboard, and now they were a creamy white while the hardwood floor gleamed. The star on the Christmas tree in front of the window almost touched the ceiling.

This house looked like a home now. Disquieted, Bran realized it had come to feel more like home to him than his own apartment did. He had dinner here at least a couple times a week, and often spent one of his days off helping Zach work on the place.

Tess reappeared with two bottles of a dark German beer, smiled and said, "I'll leave you two to talk."

"No, you can hear this unless there's something you want to get back to," he heard himself say.

"Of course I want to hear." She plopped down on the sofa next to Zach, who wrapped an arm around her.

At first sight, anyone would have been able to tell the two men were brothers. Both were an inch or two above six feet, athletic. Zach's features were cleaner cut, making him handsome and Bran…not. At least in his opinion. Zach had dark hair, Bran a deep auburn darkened from the carrot-red he'd been born with. Both had blue eyes the same color as their mother's, a fact that disconcerted Bran when he thought about it. He'd turned his back on her a lot of years ago and still wasn't happy to have been forced to accept her in his life. Again, because of Zach.

Tess was a cross between sex goddess and girl-next-door with her scattering of freckles. She was tall enough to have modeled, had thick, glossy, maple-brown hair and green-gold eyes. Bran wasn't oblivious to her sexual appeal, but hadn't been slammed with it at first sight the way his brother was. Good thing, as it turned out.

Now Lina, she'd hit him hard. If he'd had her number, he'd have called her within twenty-four hours. Truth was, he hadn't so much as touched another woman since the night with Lina. He had convinced himself it was because of Paige and the last-minute cancellation of their wedding, but he knew better now. He hadn't been able to get Lina out of his head.

Nobody said a word. Their expectant expressions spoke for them.

He groaned and tugged at his hair, which was more characteristic of Zach than him. Getting started wasn't easy. "The night before my wedding—what should have been my wedding— I got drunk."

Zach nodded, even though he, like Bran, wasn't much of a drinker.

"I should have gone home, but I didn't. I went to a tavern, and I met a woman. We spent the night together, but I didn't know anything but her first name. When I got out of the shower in the morning, she had taken off."

"With your wallet?" his brother, the cop, asked.

"No. She hadn't touched anything. I made some attempt to find her, but with only a first name, I struck out." He hesitated, suddenly wishing he hadn't invited Tess to sit in on this confession. "I didn't use a condom."

"Oh, dear," she said.

He grimaced. "The one solid witness to today's bank robbery? It's her. Lina. Lina Jurick. And she's six months pregnant."

Zach swore.

"She didn't know how to find you, either?"

That was Tess, optimistic about human nature.

"She knew," he said grimly. "Turns out, I'd had the damn wedding invitation with me. While I was in the shower, she saw it. That's why she took off."

"O-oh," Tess breathed.

"She swears she was going to tell me before the baby was born. It's a girl," he added. "What it comes down to is, I'm going to be a father."

"Shouldn't you insist on some testing?" his brother asked. "To be sure you *are* the father?"

Bran shook his head, sure at least about this much. "Lina isn't like that. She teaches at the middle school. She's a thoroughly nice woman."

"Pretty?"

"Beautiful." He rubbed a hand over his jaw. "My head is spinning."

"How much did she see today?" Zach asked.

Bran told them about the robbery and about his own initial fear that the killer might know Lina. "Doesn't sound likely, though," he concluded. "She says he has one of those faces. Not ugly, not handsome. Not memorable. His head was shaved, and she isn't sure if he was partially bald or what. She thinks he might have had an earring but didn't see any tattoos. The feds will be sitting down with her in the morning, and the sketch artist as soon as we can line it up."

"But tomorrow is Christmas Eve."

"Yeah, that complicates things."

"So, back to Lina," his brother said. "What's your plan?"

Wheels had been grinding in his head since he'd set eyes on her at the pharmacy. "Spend time with her," he heard himself say. "Unless I don't like her, I'll marry her." He shrugged. "Why not? I intended to marry. I want a family. With her, I already have one."

Amusement glinted in Zach's eyes, but Tess gaped at him.

"Just like that?" She sounded outraged. "No special fondness required? If that's not a recipe for disaster!"

"Why would it be?" he countered. "I liked her when we talked. And we did talk quite a bit that night. We're attracted. We're having a baby together. Not so many years ago, that alone would have guaranteed a wedding."

"But it doesn't anymore. Bran, what if you fall in love with someone else? What if she does?"

He'd kill the son of a bitch, that was what. Bran blinked at the violence of his reaction to the idea. No, he decided, there was nothing surprising about it. She was carrying his baby. She was his, even if she didn't know it yet. He didn't share, and when he made a commitment, by God he kept it, and he expected the same of her.

"I'm closing in on forty," he said. "It's not happening."

"So you were drunk that night," Zach said thoughtfully, rather than asking how old Lina was. "What about her?"

Suddenly wary, Bran asked, "And that matters how?"

"She was at a tavern on her own, maybe getting plastered. Either that wasn't so unusual for her, which makes me think you should ask some more questions before she puts your name on that birth certificate, or it *was* unusual for her, in which case you have to ask yourself what was going on that had her there."

He stared at his brother, who was right. He should have asked himself exactly that. Why hadn't he? Because she seemed so nice? What kind of idiot was he?

After a minute, he nodded. "Okay."

"Does she have family in town?" Tess asked.

"No. Doesn't sound like she's going anywhere, either."

Her forehead crinkled. "She won't be by herself for Christmas, will she?"

"I don't know," he admitted. "I didn't get a straight answer." He hesitated. "The loan officer Lina saw killed? Maya Lee was her best friend."

A gasp escaped Tess, who pressed a hand to her mouth. Even Zach looked disturbed.

"She was there because they were supposed to have lunch together. In no time, it's going to occur to her that, if she'd suggested an earlier time, her friend would be alive. Or she'll come up with some other reason to start blaming herself. I told her she's going to have nightmares," Bran said. "I didn't like leaving her, but I didn't have a lot of choices."

"Do you think she'd join us tomorrow night?" Tess asked immediately, with the generosity he'd come to expect of her.

"Your dad will be here." Not, thank God, his mother, who had plans with her current husband—number five—and stepkids. Bran would have preferred never to see her again, but he had been polite at Zach's wedding. He wasn't looking forward to the next time he had to be polite to her.

"So?"

"I don't know, Tess. I'll…think about it. She may not want to."

"She's going to be the mother of your daughter, no matter what. That makes her family, in a way."

"I told her that, but I don't think she's quite over finding out why I was there getting plastered that night. She was offended to think I was supposed to get married the next morning. I think she figures she was some sort of stand-in."

His brother's eyebrows rose. "Wasn't she?"

Bran scowled. "No."

His brother smiled. "You being mad and depressed didn't have anything to do with you taking a woman you didn't know to bed."

"I wasn't depressed." He didn't deny the mad part. "I had no intention of picking up a woman. All I wanted was a few drinks. She and I hit it off. That didn't have anything to do with the damn wedding."

Zach's smile widened. "Then bring her tomorrow. Let us meet her."

He sighed and took the first swallow of his beer. "I'll try."

Zach asked about Mrs. Greaver and Bran's appointment to see her this afternoon. He had, at least, thought to call her instead of being a no-show. She'd sounded the tiniest bit relieved.

"If you're tied up with this bank robbery, I can get in touch with her," Zach offered. "Or has the FBI taken over the whole show?"

"Actually, these two haven't been bad to work with. They seem to want to collaborate."

His brother grinned. "You mean, they need minions to do their bidding, don't they?"

Despite his mood, Bran grunted a laugh. "Probably."

Not until he left half an hour later did he wonder if he hadn't stopped by to see Zach and Tess because he was hoping they'd suggest he bring Lina. Something about that small tree with only a few presents under it in Lina's apartment had saddened Bran, damn it, even though he wasn't big on holidays himself. This year, he hadn't bothered to decorate because he wouldn't be spending Christmas Eve or Day at his own place. Last year, he'd been stuck joining Paige's family. The year before, he ignored the holiday. This year was different. He had family again.

Discovering he was being driven by impulses lurking in his subconscious didn't make him happy. He used his head; he didn't make decisions because of emotions.

And, sure, he'd surprised himself with the announcement that he was going to marry Lina, but the decision itself was entirely rational. It disturbed him a little that his equally rational decision to marry Paige had blown up in his face the way it did, but he was grateful now it had. Lina was a better choice. He'd have stuck to the commitment he made to Paige, but the truth was, he'd been finding he didn't much like her as the wedding neared.

When she called it off, he'd been mad as hell. He'd never imagined himself in love with her, so it had been his pride that took the hit. Driving through the dark streets on the way back to his lonely apartment tonight, he admitted to himself for the first time that she had made the right choice for both of them. She wanted more than he could give. What he'd never seen before was that he had wanted more than she had to give, too.

Something was happening inside him, and it didn't feel good. His chest felt compressed as he tried to figure out what it was he did want, beyond wife and kids. Home.

He didn't have an answer.

THE PAIR OF FBI agents came to Lina's apartment. Never having met a real, live FBI agent, she felt intimidated as she let them in. One was a woman, which helped her relax. Probably in her forties, the first thing she asked was when Lina was due. The man, way younger, appeared increasingly uncomfortable as the two women discussed pregnancy and childbirth.

He finally growled, "Can we get on with it?"

His partner grinned. "Scared you, did we?"

They did get down to business, making Lina repeat everything she'd already told Bran and then some. They asked some good questions. She was able to make what she thought was a pretty accurate estimate of height for the robber who had shot Maya. She remembered that mud had splattered the tires and bottom of the doors and sides of the cargo van, something she didn't think she'd told Bran.

"It looked recent," she said, thinking it out. "I mean, it was dry, or mostly dry anyway, but if they'd driven for hours I'd have thought more of it would have fallen off. You know? It had to have been from the day before, when it rained."

"It might have rained here, but it didn't in Seattle," Agent Novinski, the woman, said flatly. She took out her phone and did a search. "Or in Tacoma."

"Ruts and holes on a dirt road can stay muddy for quite a while, though," Lina pointed out.

"That's true," Novinski agreed, but Lina could tell she wasn't satisfied.

They wanted a better description of both the men than she could give them. No, she had no idea what color the second man's eyes were. He had been looking at Mr. Floyd, not toward her. Wiry, short for a man. She was sure the hand that held the gun was encased in the kind of thin glove doctors and nurses wore.

They were even more dissatisfied when she

couldn't be sure what color eyes the guy who'd shot Maya had.

"But you say he stared right at you," the male agent said.

"Yes, but you know how thick the glass is, and I was looking through it at an angle. Plus, I'd just seen my best friend get shot." She glared at both of them. "It was horrible. Do you know what happens when somebody gets shot in the head?"

Clearly they did. Special Agent Novinski, the woman, had the grace to appear regretful.

"I was beyond shocked, and terrified, too. I can still see his face and the way he looked at me, but I didn't think, oh, he has blue eyes."

Naturally, at that moment she pictured Bran Murphy's eyes, a vivid blue. She wished, quite passionately, that he was here. He wouldn't let these two badger her.

"My best guess is hazel or light brown. You know, kind of in between." She frowned. "I don't think he had really dark hair, either. Even shaved, his head would have looked different if he did. His jaw would have been darker, too. He was definitely Caucasian." She spread her hands in a helpless gesture. "I looked at him for a total of maybe ten seconds. This is the best I can do."

Eventually they gave up and departed, leaving her feeling drained. Lunch might help, she thought, but didn't move. Even making a sandwich seemed like a herculean effort. She wished suddenly, selfishly, that she had gone home for Christmas. Maya would still be dead, but her death wouldn't be so brutally real. Lina wouldn't be the only person who could potentially identify one of the men who'd robbed at least three banks.

And, oh, yeah, she'd still be in deep avoidance about telling Bran he was going to be a father.

Her phone rang. His name came up. For some reason, she didn't hesitate to answer the call.

"Are they done with you?" he asked.

Stung, she said, "Hi. Yes, I'm fine this morning. Thank you for asking."

There was a short silence. "Are you really fine?" he asked, in a different voice.

"No." She closed her eyes. "I mean, yes, I'm okay."

"Have they come and gone?"

"Yes. I don't think I satisfied them, but I can't see through walls and ski masks, so they were bound to be disappointed."

"They were hopeful." Was that a smile in his voice? "Can I bring you lunch?"

Her stomach came to attention. "What kind of lunch?"

"I was thinking pizza, but if you'd rather I could stop for deli sandwiches."

In the interests of not gaining too much weight, Lina tried not to indulge often, but pizza sounded like exactly what she needed right now. "I would love pizza," she admitted. "Can you make mine half veggie?"

"You don't eat meat?"

"I just want to know I'm eating something healthy along with all the fat, okay?"

She heard a rusty sound that might be a chuckle. "Good thinking. Give me half an hour."

And he was gone.

"I DON'T LIKE the sound of that," he said flatly.

"Of mud?" Lina seemed bemused. "Why?"

He had set down his slice of pizza, wiped off his fingers and quickly checked his phone, to find that the last rain in south King County or Pierce County had been eight days earlier.

"Because it suggests they were staying up here for at least the previous day. They wouldn't have picked up mud on the highway or in town." The bank was actually outside the city limits because of recent growth the Clear Creek council members hadn't been farsighted enough to anticipate, to their current frustration over lost tax dollars. A good percent of homes in the rural county were on dirt or gravel roads that developed potholes and ruts. Very few homes on acreage had paved driveways, either.

"Well, doesn't that make sense anyway?"

Lina asked. "I mean, Tacoma to here is kind of a long commute."

He gave her a look she ignored. After two slices of pizza, she was full, which left her free to speculate.

"Plus," she continued, "surely they'd have wanted to, I don't know, scope out the bank in advance. Why did they pick that bank and not Chase or Opus or Whidbey Island Bank?"

He sighed. Starting at the crack of dawn, he'd watched videos from another local bank until his eyes were crossing. Charlie was doing the same, as were several borrowed deputies. The FBI had generously taken the footage from the bank that had been robbed. They'd let the locals waste time on banks the pair hadn't targeted.

"You're right. We're going back a couple of days, thinking we'll see the same face appearing at a couple of other banks. They are unlikely to have gone in together, because two men would draw more attention than one alone."

"What if one of them was in Snoqualmie Community," she suggested, "oh, ages ago and knew the layout was perfect and the only window on the street looks in at a conference room instead of the bank proper?"

"But why would he have been if he's not a local?"

"He has a girlfriend or just a friend up here

who needed to stop at the bank one day when they were together? He'd go in out of professional curiosity, wouldn't he?"

Bran did not want to believe either of those slugs had any reason to feel at home in Harris County, because if that was the case, the likelihood became greater that he had somehow encountered Lina and that the spark of familiarity she felt was because she had actually encountered the creep.

"We have to look," he said.

"I know." Sitting cross-legged on the sofa, she made a face. "I'm sorry. You know what you're doing. I won't think of anything you haven't already considered."

He braced himself. "I don't mind hearing ideas, but that's not what I'm here to talk to you about."

Her wariness showed. So did her belly. He was still shocked at the way arousal had slammed him when she opened the door. Not once had he ever noticed a pregnant woman at the grocery store and thought, *Wow, she's sexy*. Apparently Lina was different.

Part of it, he guessed, was the fact that she was carrying *his* baby. And then there were all the memories of that night, and especially of the morning when he'd made her pregnant. God, it had been amazing. He'd never felt anything like that before.

Also, unlike the day before, she wasn't making any effort to disguise her pregnancy. No coat or thigh-length sweater. Nope, over black leggings she wore a stretchy black top that clung like a second skin to the generous curves of her body. Maybe she'd planned to do yoga or something. Her feet were bare, too. He kept finding himself fascinated by her long toes and high arches. With the nails unpainted, her feet looked innocent. Maybe she couldn't reach them anymore, it occurred to him.

Her cheeks were turning pink, which meant he was staring.

He felt some heat in his own face. "Do you have plans tonight?"

"Why?"

"Because my brother and sister-in-law suggested you join us for dinner."

Her mouth fell open. "You told them about me?"

"Shouldn't I have?"

"I don't know! We haven't decided anything!"

"You decided to admit that you're pregnant with my child."

"*Yours?* Like you *own* her?"

"You know that's not what I mean," he said, exasperated. Why would she flip out because he'd told his brother she was pregnant?

Her eyes narrowed. "Did you tell them how it happened?"

Until this minute, it hadn't occurred to him that she might mind, and why. Oh, crap. Should he lie? Be honest?

No lies, he decided, not ever. "I did," he admitted.

Lina's glare felt like the midday, equatorial sun. He'd wake up in pain tomorrow. Her voice, in contrast, was exquisitely polite if also steely. "Then you may tell them thank you, that I appreciate their kindness, but no, I can't join them tonight."

He had to fix this. "They're not judgmental people, Lina. Once they knew your due date, they'd have figured out when you got pregnant. That alone would tell them I'd done something stupid."

"Which stupid thing are you talking about? Not wearing a condom? Or did you mean, being careless enough to leave the wedding invitation lying in plain sight? But wait. Maybe you did that on purpose to make sure I didn't hang around with any illusions, like hoping that we'd just had a beautiful beginning."

"We did have a beautiful beginning," he snapped, then was shocked when he realized what he'd said. But he tried to be honest with himself, and he'd felt something unfamiliar that morning.

The timing might have sucked, but the woman and he had meshed in a whole lot of ways.

She blinked a couple times, obviously taken aback. "Why would you say that?"

Bran rolled his shoulders. "Because it's true. I don't make a habit of picking up women in bars. Yeah, I had too much to drink, and yeah, having Paige dump me at the last minute like that stung, but that's not why I wanted you. You're beautiful, and you seemed sad, and I liked you." He felt awkward. "I would have asked you out if you'd still been there when I came out of the bathroom."

"Oh." Lina nibbled on her lower lip for a moment. Her gaze shied away from his momentarily before connecting again. "I would have said yes."

"Good." It was too soon to suggest marriage, even if he'd like to have it settled. His plan to create a family had stumbled over an obstacle, but now he had another chance. One he liked even better.

One step at a time, he told himself. Zach was right, he'd need to find out why *she'd* gotten drunk and had sex with a stranger. This wasn't the moment, though, especially not if he wanted to spend Christmas Eve with her.

So, keeping his voice gentle, he said, "You didn't answer my question about tonight. Do you have plans?"

After a moment, she shook her head.

"Then won't you come with me to Zach's? I'd really like you to get to know my brother and sister-in-law."

She searched his eyes, her own betraying more vulnerability than she'd probably like. "Are you sure I'm welcome?"

"I'm sure."

Her knotted hands clenched and tightened a couple times. "Okay. I admit, I wasn't looking forward to tonight, especially not after...you know."

He nodded. "I do know. Uh... I'd better get back to work. I'll pick you up at five thirty, if that works."

"Thank you," she said with dignity. "Can I bring anything? I mean, food?"

He guessed there'd be plenty, but he said, "Don't rush out to the grocery store, but if there's a dish you can make easily, Tess would probably appreciate it. I know she's baking a ham."

She told him she'd think of something, and escorted him to the door. Bran wanted to touch her, but the way she held herself aloof told him that wouldn't be smart. *Soon*, he told himself. He'd just achieved a significant win. He shouldn't get greedy.

CHAPTER FIVE

"I'LL HELP YOU clear the table." Lina pushed back her chair and began gathering dirty dishes before anyone could argue.

But as it happened, none of the men, which included Tess's father, leaped up and insisted that in fairness they should handle the cleanup.

Already holding two empty serving dishes, Tess smiled. "Thank you."

In the kitchen, Lina said, "I suppose you cooked the entire meal."

Tess laughed. "I did. To be fair, though, Zach worked a shift today, while I stayed home. My partner and I decided not to open the store. Who was going to shop for carpet on Christmas Eve?"

Lina had learned that Tess was half owner of Fabulous Interiors, which offered flooring, window coverings, tile and more. The house Tess and Zach were still restoring had benefited from her ability to buy materials at cost. The gorgeous tile in the bathroom was a good example. Lina had had several opportunities to admire it and the claw-footed tub. As frequently as she needed a bathroom now, she was afraid she might as well move into one the last month.

Bran had told her that Zach was also a sheriff's deputy. He was probably lucky not to be out patrolling this evening. Law-enforcement agencies couldn't shut down for holidays.

"I like your dad," she said tentatively. He'd been positively courtly to her.

"I'm glad. I feel lucky to have him." Tess glanced over her shoulder and then lowered her voice. "He had a massive stroke almost three years ago. Rehab was slow, and I keep waiting for him to have another one. I feel blessed every day he's still here."

"That must keep you on edge. He looks good, though."

"He does," Tess agreed. "Better all the time."

"It seems like he and Zach are good friends."

"They are." She laughed. "Now."

Lina returned to get another load of dirty dishes while Tess started rinsing off plates and loading the dishwasher. Lina was feeling increasingly comfortable with the woman who, it had occurred to her during the evening, would be her baby's aunt.

"I'm glad you're here," Tess said unexpectedly, after she'd started to slice two of the pies. "Bran is so alone."

"Do you think so?" Lina asked, startled. "I

would have said he's guarded, but he's been…"
How to put it? "More generous and open than I
expected, I guess. I thought he'd be mad at me
for not telling him right away about the baby."

"I'll bet you could hardly wait to have *that*
conversation."

"It was like staring up at Mount Everest, and I
was supposed to climb it without oxygen."

They were both giggling when Bran appeared
in the kitchen. He eyed them cautiously. "Tell me
you weren't talking about me."

They laughed again.

With a glint in his eyes that might have been
humor, he asked if the coffee was ready.

"It is," his sister-in-law said. "I'll pour if you'll
go take orders for pie."

"Do you have ice cream?" he asked hopefully.

Tess patted his cheek. "Of course I do." She
paused for a moment, watching him go. "He's
loosening up."

"What do you mean?"

"I don't think he liked me at first. Or he didn't
want to like me. Or he liked me, but didn't know
how to show he did. Or—" She made a face. "I
feel as if I still don't really know him. He and
Zach have reasons for not being very trusting—"
At the sound of footfalls, she broke off.

"Two blueberry, one apple," Bran reported.
"Ice cream all around."

The women decided to each try the other's pie.

The men had been talking about college football and the upcoming bowl games when the women served them, but lost interest the minute they had forks in their hands.

"I like football," Lina said into the silence as they dug into the pie. "Mostly pro. Since I grew up in Minnesota…"

The men all groaned.

Eventually, they got around to talking about the next day. Zach was working the day shift again. With not much seniority, he hadn't been given a choice. He shrugged. "I'd have volunteered anyway. The guys with kids should have the holiday off. We can celebrate anytime."

"We're planning to gorge again tomorrow night," Tess said cheerfully. "I have a humongous turkey and we'll open our presents after dinner. Please join us, Lina."

She groped for a polite out. Her daughter might be family, but she wasn't. "That's kind of you, but I can't."

Bran's hand found hers under the table. "Please," he said softly.

Face burning, Lina looked around to see only friendly, encouraging expressions. Why were they being so nice to a woman Bran had picked up in a bar, for heaven's sake? But she knew.

However they felt about her, she was carrying Bran's baby.

"I can't," she repeated. "I haven't had a chance to buy gifts for any of you, and—"

"And we haven't for you, either," Tess said briskly. "But I can't stand to think of you alone tomorrow night."

Isabel had invited her to join her family, too, but Lina had already declined. It was better to be alone than feel like an outsider.

Although, somehow she hadn't felt like an outsider tonight. She thought it was possible she and Tess might become friends. And Bran was either an amazing actor, or he really wanted her to say yes.

After a moment, she smiled shakily. "Then thank you. This is really nice of you."

Bran squeezed her hand, but didn't let go of it. He rotated his coffee cup so he could pick it up with his left hand. Lina wondered if anyone else had noticed. She ought to tug her hand free, but couldn't make herself. How funny that she hadn't realized until this moment how alone *she* had felt, good friends notwithstanding.

The prospect of becoming a single mother was daunting. She'd have more support if she moved back home, but she hadn't seriously considered it. She loved her job and her coworkers, she liked Clear Creek, she didn't miss Minnesota winters and she hadn't felt close to her parents in a long while. She'd opened the distance because they hadn't liked David, and her mother, in particular, couldn't resist reminding her every single time they talked that she should have listened to them.

Yes, they'd been right and she'd been wrong, but she didn't need to hear it over and over and over. And now, an unplanned pregnancy and her being unmarried... Even though she *claimed* she was excited about her first grandchild, Mom would still be going on about the unmarried thing when Lina's daughter was accepting her college diploma.

Astonishingly, her baby had a father now. None of Lina's fears had materialized, at least not yet. The generosity of Bran's family astonished her. Tess, she thought, was genuine. Zach, Lina was less sure of, except that he'd been polite.

No, she couldn't entirely believe in all of this, but right now, at least...she didn't feel alone. And that was a gift.

CHRISTMAS HAD GONE WELL. Bran couldn't have planned it better if he'd been able to stage the whole thing. He'd seen Lina relax, minute by minute. Family was just what he'd needed to swing her to his point of view.

The twenty-sixth being a Saturday, Bran was at his desk. He'd gone in, hoping Novinski would have sent him the files she'd promised on the other robberies, but apparently she had taken the holiday off. Today, she'd loaded his inbox.

Warring had shown up today, too, as much a workaholic as Bran, and for the same reason. No wife, no live-in girlfriend, no kids. The thought drifted through Bran's head that he might change, but he shook it off. The threat to Lina, however improbable, had to be his priority.

"Good holiday?" Charlie asked, sitting down at the next desk with a cup of coffee.

"Yeah, it was." Surprisingly, he meant it. He had managed to buy Lina a present, which had both embarrassed and pleased her, if he was any judge. He'd stopped the afternoon of Christmas Eve at a jeweler and found a gold pendant that, with simple, almost abstract lines, depicted a man embracing a woman and baby. Bran's message wasn't subtle. "Had it with Zach and his wife," he said. And Lina. People would learn about the baby eventually, but he hoped to be engaged to her before then. "You?"

"My parents. They live in Seattle. My sister and her family were there, too." Charlie shrugged. "Her four-year-old thought Christmas morning was the greatest thing ever."

Bran's heart contracted hard, the sensation almost painful. Next Christmas, he'd have a kid of his own. Every once in a while, the reality of it hit him.

He forwarded some of the files to Charlie's email box, and they started to read. Bran, at least, was grimly determined.

It didn't take him half an hour to discover he concurred with the opinion of the feds: the same two men were responsible for at least five robberies besides the most recent. The first one, they'd made off with about $15,000, hastily gathered by a teller. The timing had been good enough after an armored car had arrived with cash at the Bank of America in Tacoma, they'd gotten away with nearly $100,000. The others were amounts in between, but altogether added up to damn near $300,000. Divided in half, though, that didn't make them rich men these days, which meant they were probably already planning their next job. The fact that they had killed people this time might make them nervous enough to take a longer than usual break—or getting away with it could have gone to their heads. They were already wanted not only for bank robbery but also for murder. What did they have to lose now?

His concentration wasn't as absolute as usual. Lina hadn't said what she would be doing today beyond her intention to swim laps at the high school pool. He didn't like the idea of her out and about even if common sense suggested that the last thing the two robbers would do was hang around Clear Creek. Unless they knew Lina's name, of course, but how could they? Even so, it wouldn't hurt for him to call and check in with her a couple of times.

He also couldn't forget that Mrs. Greaver, the neighbor from when he was a kid, had agreed to meet with Zach today. Talking to the woman on the phone, Zach, too, had sensed her reluctance. Were they about to catch a break?

Nothing about investigating their sister's murder had been pleasant. Zach, only nine years old when it happened, had been the one to discover Sheila's body. He would never be able to wipe that memory out of his head.

Their pretty, unfailingly happy sister had been raped and strangled when she was only six. The police had suspected Michael Murphy, Bran and Zach's father, if only because they had failed to come up with any other viable suspect. They had trouble believing that anyone could have sneaked into the house and taken Sheila out the back door without waking either of her parents, whose bedroom had been right next to Sheila's.

The marriage didn't last long after that. Bran had overheard enough of his parents' arguments to know they had thrown terrible accusations at each other. What marriage could survive that? Bran had already known that his mother was sleeping around, too. In the heated weeks following Sheila's murder, it became apparent that Bran's dad knew, as well, or had at least suspected.

In the end, a great divide opened. The boys had had to choose which parent they wanted to live with. Bran's bitterness about his mother's infidelity guaranteed he would choose Dad; Zach, who refused to believe Mom was anything but saintly, had chosen her. Turned out there was an added factor: he'd heard their father get up during the night of Sheila's death, although he told the police he'd never stirred.

Because of the lie, Zach had always believed their dad was the killer, too.

There'd been calls and letters and gifts at first, but contact slowed to a trickle by the end of the first year, then ended completely.

When the brothers had met up again this past spring, their divided loyalties had spilled over into their relationship. Mending it had meant keeping an open mind about who the killer could have been. Unfortunately, every trail they'd followed so far had dead-ended, however promising it initially seemed.

Most recently, they had been looking hard at men who'd been teenagers at the time of the murder.

"Crap," Bran said out loud. "I'm going to print

all this and take it home. The manager of the Bank of America agreed to meet me there today so I can watch more videos. I still have a couple days' worth to go."

Charlie stretched and groaned. "Sounds like a plan. Maybe I can do the same if I can get in touch with anyone to let me in." He'd taken Wells Fargo. "But damn, I keep thinking these assholes might have cased the banks two weeks ago. A month ago. Who knows? We could be wasting our time completely sticking to just the last week."

"But how practical is it for us to watch a month's worth of videos at every bank in town?" Bran countered. "And that's assuming they even have that far back. Why would they store more than a week or two?"

"Just saying."

"I don't like anything about this," Bran said shortly, and strode to the printer to start collecting the reams it was spitting out.

THE FIRST THING Mrs. Greaver said was, "It really is you." She looked shocked.

Zach laughed at that. "You thought I was lying about who I am?"

"I just don't understand why you're back in town." She let him inside. "You left a long time ago."

"Twenty-five years," he agreed, assessing the

small living room crammed with too much furniture. The drapes were closed, the light dim. He'd heard the television before he rang the doorbell.

As a kid, he'd been in and out of some of the other homes on the block, but not the Greavers' as far as he could remember. Their kids were older than the Murphy gang; they didn't play together. He'd known the daughter best, as she'd babysat them.

When he asked about Mary, Mrs. Greaver led him to the photos on the fireplace mantel. Studying them, he would have recognized his former babysitter anywhere. Like her mother, she had remained scrawny and short, with a foxy face and tight mouth. Mary hadn't loved babysitting, no secret about that. Or else she just hadn't liked the Murphy boys. She looked all buttoned up as an adult, too, though, so maybe that was just her.

The Greavers' son, Zach hardly recalled. Rob was a couple years younger than Mary, apparently, which would have made him around fifteen when Sheila was killed and Zach's family imploded. Bran, twelve then, remembered him better than Zach did, which was why their original plan had been for Bran to take this interview.

Mrs. Greaver asked about Bran, and Zach explained that he was the detective in charge of investigating the bank robbery, which was consuming his days. He didn't mention that the one witness was a woman who was pregnant with Bran's baby.

Zach learned more than he wanted to about Mary, who lived in Yakima now, on the eastern side of the mountains, was married and had two kids. Mary's oldest had joined the air force right out of high school. Momentarily stupefied, Zach thought, *Wait. Was that possible?* With a little calculating, he figured out that she must have had the kid right out of high school.

Funny thing, though, Mrs. Greaver didn't volunteer a word about Rob. Zach had to ask. He'd been married and divorced, his mother said. No children. Her mouth closed tightly. When prodded, she said he was in Seattle and drove trucks for a living.

Zach knew better than to push right out of the gate. Years as a cop had taught him how to get someone to open up. He told a funny story about Mary when she was taking care of him and Sheila. Bran must have been at a friend's, because he wasn't in that memory. Mrs. Greaver reminded Zach tartly of a few of his and Bran's more infamous escapades. Only gradually did he bring Sheila into the conversation. By that time, Mrs. Greaver seemed to have forgotten he'd ever moved away from the neighborhood.

"The reason we wanted to talk to you," he said at last, "is because your kids were older than Bran and me. We figured if anyone knew all the teenagers in the neighborhood, it would be you."

Instead of preening as he'd expected—people liked being considered an expert—she said grudgingly, "I suppose I did."

"I'm sure you'd have told the investigating officers at the time if you'd been aware of any older boys in the neighborhood who had seemed interested in Sheila," he said. "But it's possible you've remembered something since that might help us find out who killed her. Twenty-five years ago, the detectives probably didn't even consider a teenage boy could have done it. They were looking for an adult. But times have changed."

As he talked, her expression had become downright hostile. "From what *I* heard, the police believed your father killed that poor little girl. You may not believe that, but it doesn't excuse you wanting to shift the blame to people just because they lived nearby."

So much for softening her up.

"Mrs. Greaver, you must watch the news. There've been several ugly cases in the past year alone of boys who were only fourteen or fifteen years old sexually assaulting and murdering a younger girl. It happens. I'm hoping you can give me names of any boys who were around then. I'm not conducting a witch hunt, but one of them might have been arrested in the intervening years for something that will raise a red flag. None of them will ever even know I've run their names unless they become a person of interest."

Her spine stiffened. "Your sister is long gone. Why don't you let her rest in peace?"

He nodded and rose to his feet. "I'm sorry if I've upset you, Mrs. Greaver. I didn't want to do that. I can only remind you that Sheila was the victim. I loved my little sister. She was the sweetest kid in the world." Even after all this time, his throat tightened. "She didn't deserve what happened to her. Just think about this—how many other little girls has that man hurt in all the years since then?"

She didn't respond, or even stand to see him out. When he left, she was still sitting on her sofa, hands clasped tightly on her lap, looking straight ahead at the fireplace and all those family pictures—none of which included an adult Rob Greaver.

WHEN FIRST PROMOTED to detective, Bran had had no idea how much of his time would be spent watching piss-poor footage from surveillance cameras. Or how grateful he'd be that it existed at all, grainy and poorly lit or not. Half the time, it would turn out that the camera pointing right at a crime scene or escape vehicle hadn't worked in years. The business owner had been sure criminals would be scared off by the sight of a camera, functional or not.

Three hours after sitting in an office at the bank to watch the less than riveting action from two days before the robbery, Bran found his vision already blurring. He'd never given any thought to how busy banks were. The Bank of America didn't seem to have much in the way of lulls. Not many chances to fast-forward or let his mind wander. Thank God he didn't also have to watch footage from the camera outside that pointed at the ATM.

A fair number of the customers he saw coming and going appeared familiar to him. Clear Creek was the largest city in the county, but that wasn't saying much. In many ways, it functioned as a small town. Everyone knew everyone else.

He rewound a couple of times when someone behaved oddly, then shrugged and went on. The manager, who couldn't leave him alone in the bank, had gotten the coffee machine going and kept his cup filled, which he appreciated. So far, every bank officer in town had been completely cooperative. They were all but doing somersaults in their efforts to help. They knew damn well they'd dodged a bullet when the pair chose to rob a different bank. Outside urban areas, it was easy to get complacent about security. A whole bunch of people had just been awakened to frightening reality.

After rubbing his eyes, he watched as a woman with two toddlers came in, saw a line and turned right around to go out. A man politely held open the door for her and proceeded to one of the self-help counters. Beneath a parka he wore a gray, hooded sweatshirt. The fact that he didn't push the hood back had Bran sitting up. Then he stiffened as he saw how careful the guy was to keep his face averted from the cameras, the way he kept his chin tucked in to achieve maximum coverage from the hood. He took his time, filling out some kind of a deposit or withdrawal slip, but his head kept turning. Oh, yeah, he was looking around. After a minute, he ostentatiously patted his hip pocket but came up empty. Then the pockets in his parka. Nobody seemed to be paying any attention to him. He thrust the deposit slip in one of those pockets, then went to the display stand to grab a brochure. Finally, he strolled out, without once letting the camera capture his face full-on or even close to it.

Damn, Bran thought. They could, and should, use this video for training bank employees. *This is what you should watch for.*

From his size, this guy wasn't the one who'd shot Maya Lee. He was the partner, described by Lina as lean, wiry and not very tall. Bran went back several minutes to watch the same footage again in slow motion, freezing it a couple of times when he glimpsed the line of the guy's jaw or cheek. The IT people might be able to do something with this. The man had been wearing gloves when he opened the door, but stripped them off as soon as he was inside. It would have looked too odd if he hadn't. He didn't make a single slipup, though, using a pen he produced from his pocket and taking the only piece of paper he'd touched with him when he left, his back to the camera. Sure as hell, he had put his gloves back on before he pulled open the door.

It was frustrating, but more than they'd had. As Bran called Novinski, it occurred to him he'd be watching the camera positioned outside above the ATM after all. The guy probably hadn't parked in the bank lot, but everyone made a mistake eventually.

Of the two, he speculated, was this the brains of the outfit? The boss, responsible for making the decision on which bank was their best target? Or had they divided up the task of evaluating the possibilities and made the final decision democratically?

The FBI agent came on the line. "What's up?"

"I found one of them on camera at the Bank of America. No good look at the face, but someone with the skill might be able to do something with the video."

Another call came in before they finished talking. Charlie.

"Let me call you back in a minute," Bran said, and switched to his partner.

"Found him," Charlie said.

They compared dates and time. The visit to Bank of America had come first. An hour later, what had to be the same man had checked out Wells Fargo.

"Can't see his face," Charlie said in frustration, "but at least we know when they were in town. With only a few days in between, it's possible they stayed until the heist. I'm going to talk to bank personnel, just in case this guy caught someone's eye. If anyone saw him get in a vehicle…"

They both knew that was a pipe dream, but Bran would do the same. They had to try.

Calling Novinski back, Bran found himself wondering where Lina was right now. Then, irritated with himself, he made the effort to shove her out of his head. A distracted man could miss something important.

LINA MISSED BEING able to get in the hot tub after doing her laps, a no-no according to her doctor, but she felt wonderful anyway as she wrapped her wet suit in her towel and dropped both along with her goggles into her plastic-lined tote bag. Gotta love those endorphins. This was the most relaxed she'd felt since seeing her friend's murder, and the swim had revived her after a mostly sleepless night. Wow, she should definitely come every day until school started up again.

On her way out, she exchanged greetings with a few people. The mother of one of her students stopped her to ask her *exact* due date and say how much her daughter would miss Lina when she took maternity leave. She wasn't about to explain to anyone but a close friend how very *un*planned this pregnancy had been.

She stepped into the cold, crisp air as she left the phys ed complex and started toward her car. She didn't miss Minnesota's bitter winters. Here, she didn't have to wrap a muffler around her face to keep her nose from developing frostbite in ten minutes, but the seasons were still well defined.

With the gym and weight rooms open, too, the parking lot was surprisingly crowded considering school wasn't in session. Lina paused to orient herself, then spotted her landmark, a giant tan SUV. Yep, there it was. Naturally, her little car was hidden behind it.

Almost there, Lina had a moment of panic. Before going in the pool, she'd taken off the necklace that Bran had given her for Christmas and forgotten to put it back on. The gift had been so perfect, she'd never forgive herself if she lost it.

No, no, she'd tucked it safely in her coat pocket, she calmed herself, then remembered the pea-coat had slipped off the hook and been crumpled on the bottom of the locker when she opened it. What if the necklace had fallen out and she hadn't noticed?

Relief flooded her when her delving hand found it immediately. She pulled it out, only then becoming aware a car was coming up behind her. Lina veered out of the way, seeing her car at the same moment.

Car keys. Darn it, she usually had them out already. She was about to grope for them with the same hand that already held the necklace…when she felt the fine gold chain slither out of her fingers. With a moan, she crouched to pick it up— at the exact moment she heard a strange popping sound and a metallic *ding*.

Still crouched, Lina started to swivel to see where the sounds came from, forgetting that her center of balance had altered. She was falling even as she heard a second *pop*…and felt a sharp sting on her upper arm.

Were those *gunshots*?

With a whimper, she flattened her hands on the pavement to push herself between the vehicles.

She heard raised voices followed by the pounding of running feet on pavement…and the roar of a vehicle accelerating away.

CHAPTER SIX

THE BANK MANAGER had somehow sent the relevant minutes of digital images to the IT people at the Seattle FBI office. Bran had no idea how and wasn't sure he wanted to know. Probably he should strive to be more tech savvy, but the skills were rarely required for his investigations.

His phone rang when he was shaking the manager's hand, on the verge of leaving. Seeing Lina's name, Bran said, "Excuse me. I need to take this," and pushed through the exit to the parking lot. "Lina?"

"Somebody just, um, shot at me." She sounded shaky. "At least, we think…"

A fireball exploded in his chest. "Are you hurt?"

"Not really. I skinned my knees and my hands, and a bullet grazed my arm, but it's not much more than a scratch." She almost pulled off a laugh. "Who knew I'd ever get to say that."

"A scratch," he repeated, unable to move past what she'd just said. Someone had shot at her. She'd been grazed by a bullet.

"There's a deputy here," she added. "Do you want to talk to him?"

Already unlocking his car, he said, "Yes."

"Detective Murphy? This is Dan Elkins. Ms. Jurick thinks this incident may be related to your investigation."

Backing out of the parking slot, Bran asked, "Where are you?"

"What? Oh, the high school. She was walking out to her car after swimming laps."

He switched to hands-free, distantly surprised that he was functioning. A sort of autopilot had taken over. "I'm on my way," he said curtly. "Tell me what happened."

At least two shots had been fired, likely from a car. Lina said they sounded more like a pop than the crack that she expected from gunfire. By sheer chance, she had bent over suddenly to pick something up just as the first shot was fired. Startled, she had lost her balance and fallen, causing the second shot to miss, as well.

In other words, she'd been saved by a freakin' miracle. Two miracles.

Bran turned on the lights and siren, driving as fast as he dared. On the way, he heard more of the story.

Two men coming out of the gym had seen the car idling as well as Lina's tumble. Upon hearing what one of them recognized as shots, they had come running. The shooter had presumably seen them, because the car took off. One of the men was an off-duty firefighter, Elkins explained, the other a soldier home on leave.

Through the phone, Bran heard a siren cut off. "Paramedics are just arriving," the deputy said unnecessarily.

"Tell Lina I'll be there momentarily." Able to see the high school ahead, he ended the call. Fear and rage burned in him. Lina could have been killed, just like that. Gone. The thought was unendurable.

He shouldn't have bought into assumptions the FBI agents had made. He'd seen Lina's hesitation when he asked if she recognized the man who had killed her friend. He remembered what she'd said, word for word.

He might just have had an ordinary face, but it's like, oh, if you see someone out of context and can't place them. They're a stranger, but not. You know?

But the FBI didn't believe the two were local, so he'd gone with the ordinary-face explanation— and left Lina unprotected.

This was his fault.

He pulled in behind the ambulance, where a cluster of people stood. Lina sat on the tailgate. As he got out of his county car, he heard her protesting.

"Really, I'm fine. I can clean up at home—"
Her gaze fastened desperately on his and she
broke off. It was as if no one else was there. He
saw no one but her. Completely unaware of people stepping aside, Bran went straight to her, taking in the sight of the thick gauze wrapping her
upper arm and both her hands, the grit and blood
mixed with tattered fabric at her knees. Her hair
was falling out of whatever she'd used to con-
fine it.

"No," he said softly, tipping her chin up with
one hand.

"No what?"

"No, you're not cleaning up at home. You're
going to the hospital." When her jaw set mul-
ishly, he shook his head. "For my sake." Then he
played dirty. "For the baby's sake."

"Oh." Bending her head, she touched her stomach with one bandaged hand. "I didn't fall that
hard. I've felt her moving since." Lina met his
eyes again. Whatever she saw must have been
persuasive, because she nodded. "Yes. Okay.
Only…"

"Only what?"

"Will you come?"

"I'll follow you there as soon as I get things
started here."

She tried to smile and to thank him.

"Damn it, Lina!" The fear kept swelling inside

him, stinging his throat and sinuses. He bent forward and gently wrapped his arms around her.

With a funny little sound, she rested her forehead on his chest. He breathed in her scent and began to believe she was all right.

But she might not have been, a voice in his head persisted in reminding him. A few inches one way or the other and she'd be dead.

Even thinking that way was like stepping off a cliff. He couldn't let himself. Not now. He had a job to do.

"Okay, sweetheart," he murmured. "You need to go get checked out. I have to interview witnesses and start a search for the bullets."

Her head bobbed against him. She straightened and they looked into each other's eyes for one naked moment. Then Bran stepped back and let the pair of paramedics settle her in the back of the ambulance.

He was turning away when she suddenly called in alarm, "Wait!" Hand moving to his weapon, he spun in place to give the surroundings a swift, hard look. What had she seen?

But nothing had changed. A few more people were coming out of the gym, all gaping at the police cars and ambulance. He focused on the ambulance where she sat up on a gurney. "What?"

"My necklace!" She sounded on the verge of tears. "It slipped out of my hand. That's why I stooped in the first place. Please find it. Please. Oh, and my bag and my keys must be on the ground, too." Those were obviously an afterthought.

Jesus, this latest spike of adrenaline had him dangerously on edge. Without a word, he walked around the back of her car and saw a brightly colored, rubberized tote bag lying on its side. When he picked it up, he found the keys under it. The necklace took him longer. He scanned the ground until a glint of gold almost beneath her back tire caught his eye. An unfamiliar emotion gripping him, he picked it up, his gaze on the pendant.

When he returned her possessions to her, Lina had tears in her eyes. She snatched the necklace out of his hand, fumbling with the clasp until the female paramedic said kindly, "I'll put it on for you. That way you can't lose it."

"Okay now?" Bran asked hoarsely.

"Yes. Thank you." Lina's lips trembled before she managed to firm them. Her shimmering eyes were enormous. He wasn't sure he could have looked away.

The male paramedic slammed the back doors, cutting off Bran's sight of her, then went around to hop in behind the wheel.

Not until the ambulance pulled away was he able to make himself move.

Then at last he focused on the uniformed dep-

uty and the two men who had saved Lina's life
by their courageous decision to run toward the
shots instead of away.

LINA HUDDLED BENEATH two thin blankets in the
small exam room. She was freezing. Probably
she was in shock, but did they have to keep it so
cold in here? And what had happened to her coat?

The wound on her upper arm really was more
of a burn. The doctor doubted it would even leave
a scar. She had been unbelievably lucky.

Earlier, her hands had actually hurt the most,
but they had been numbed so the nurse could
clean them, picking out grit, before applying a
salve and rewrapping them. Her knees stung, too,
but she'd scraped them worse plenty of times as
a kid on the playground.

She was waiting for the release papers and a
prescription for a painkiller she doubted she'd
take even if the doctor insisted it was safe for
the baby.

Through the sliding glass doors of her cubicle, she could see the nurses' station and the
tops of heads behind computer monitors. As she
watched, the doctor who had taken care of her
walked into a cubicle across the way and pulled
a curtain for privacy.

Where was Bran? She couldn't leave until he
got here. With no car, she was kind of stuck un-

less she called a friend. Maybe she should check with him. She'd bet Isabel or Sara, another teacher from her school, would come for her. Her phone should be in her tote bag. She turned her head until she spotted it, on the floor out of the way.

But at that moment her door slid open and Bran walked in, shrinking the small space in that way he had. She didn't know how he did it. At not much over six feet, he was a big man but not massive. What he had was presence. She didn't think she was the only person who'd look first at him in a crowd. Maybe it was a dominance thing, or that grim air.

His blue eyes homed in on her. "Lina."

"Hi." For the first time, she gave thought to her appearance. She could not possibly be at her best. "I think they're ready to release me," she said brightly. "Will you take me back to my car?"

He shook his head. "One of the bullets—we presume the one that grazed your arm—went into the front tire."

"You mean, I have a flat?"

"You do. But it's a little more than that. We jacked up your car and took the entire wheel. We're hoping that bullet is in better shape than the one that dinged the SUV. We found it, but it suffered some damage."

"But…when can I have my car back?" she asked in dismay.

He stood right beside the narrow bed, looking down at her, his eyes unsettlingly intense. Lina wasn't sure what his expression meant.

"Probably tomorrow, but you won't be driving it anyway until we catch these sons of bitches."

"You think…?" She couldn't make herself finish.

"We don't have a lot of drive-by shootings around here, Lina. I don't buy this was a coincidence."

She hadn't wanted to know, because if today's shooter was the man she'd seen kill Maya, that meant he *had* recognized her. He knew her name and where she lived. He must, because if he hadn't followed her to the high school, how had he found her?

"Then…when he looked familiar…"

"He was." He clenched his jaw so hard, it was a wonder his molars weren't cracking. "And I was stupid enough to disregard your gut feeling because the feds were so damn sure Pierce County was home ground for those two."

"But I don't really know him!" she cried. "At most, I've seen him somewhere. So how does *he* know who I am?"

Bran stepped even closer. She guessed he might have taken one of her hands in his if she hadn't had the blankets pulled up to her chin. "I'm going to walk you through your daily routines. We'll think about where you shop for groceries, prescription medications, shoes. Do you always go to the same gas station? You need to be thinking about parents of your students. School employees. He could be something like a janitor or bus driver. Those are the kind of people whose faces are familiar to you, even though you don't give much conscious thought to them. As a teacher, you're more visible. Once they let you out of here, that's what you and I are going to do if you feel up to it."

"I'm fine. Just…"

"Shaken up?"

"Cold," she snapped. "What did they do with my coat?"

"It was probably taken into evidence."

"Oh, wonderful." Her sudden grumpiness, Lina felt sure, was mere window-covering for the fear beneath. "It's keeping my car company."

Bran's grin took her breath away. "You should be glad neither of them are lonely."

The nurse returned then with the prescription and a couple pages of instructions for Lina to take with her. Once she'd clumsily signed her name with her gauze-wrapped hand, she was free to go.

Bran asked if they could take the blankets. He promised to return them. So it was that Lina walked out swaddled like a newborn, not much more than her nose and feet showing. It was a good thing, because the day felt a lot colder now than it had earlier. The temperature might have dropped—but she suspected shock was taking a toll, too.

Expecting a hike across the parking lot, she discovered a benefit of wearing a badge: his Camaro was parked only a few feet from the Emergency Room entrance in a spot marked For Official Vehicles Only.

"You changed cars," she said in surprise.

"I stopped by the station so I don't have to go back later."

She waited until he'd helped her ease into the passenger seat and gone around to get in himself before she asked if he was taking her home.

He paused in the act of buckling her seat belt. Of course his too-piercing blue eyes saw her every fear. "No. Lina, I'm putting you into hiding."

"But..." She stared at him. "What if you don't catch them right away? I have to go back to work a week from Monday."

"That's, what, nine days? We'll worry about it when it gets closer." He started the car, looked over his shoulder and backed out.

"Does the sheriff's department have a, well, a safe house? Or—oh, it would be the FBI, wouldn't it?" She couldn't imagine.

"Not the FBI. My call to Novinski was a waste

of time. They want to believe this shooting was random, because if it's not, that blows all their elaborate theories to shit." He sounded like he might be grinding his teeth. "Right now, we're going to my apartment so we can talk."

She felt…odd at the idea of encroaching on his personal space. Except, of course, eventually, if he chose to have visitation, she'd undoubtedly see where he lived.

She felt his occasional sidelong glance during the drive, but didn't meet it. He undermined her. Made her want something she doubted he could give. It was safer to remember that damn wedding invitation and wonder about the woman he had wanted to marry. How hurt had he been? Had he seen her since? Begged her to reconsider?

No, not that, Lina thought—it was impossible to imagine Bran Murphy begging for anything.

His apartment complex was about a mile from hers, but remarkably similar. It might even have the same owners. His unit was fourth floor, accessed via an elevator from the lobby. As soon as he let them into his apartment, she saw that the only personality in the living room came from the pair of bookcases that flanked a large-screen television. The leather sofa and recliner had to be expensive. But the plain white walls were undecorated, and being a man he hadn't bothered with knickknacks or throw pillows. *Decor* was probably not a word in his vocabulary. The living area had no windows. She'd noticed balconies; his must be accessed from one of the bedrooms.

She couldn't help noticing how spotlessly clean and orderly his place was, too. The kitchen counters were bare except for a coffee machine and a toaster. The small table was equally bare—no place mats for him. The spines of the books were perfectly aligned. Horrible man, he probably even dusted them.

"Have a seat," he said, turning the dead bolt and going straight to the thermostat, which he nudged upward. "I'll get you a sweater or something."

He disappeared down the short hall that led, she presumed, to one or maybe two bedrooms and a bathroom. He returned carrying a navy blue, hooded sweatshirt that zipped up the front.

Lina thanked him and shed the blankets. Of course she had to roll up the sleeves several times and the hem hung to midthigh, but it was cozy. She might be imagining it, but she was comforted to think his smell clung to the fabric. She heard a drawer open and close, and he came back from the kitchen with a notepad and pen. She couldn't decide whether she was relieved or sorry that he sat in the recliner instead of at the other end of the sofa.

"Damn," he said suddenly. "We forgot to fill your prescription."

"I wasn't planning to," she admitted. "Tylenol would be the best, if you have any."

He frowned, but nodded after a minute. "If you change your mind, I'll go out."

"I'll need clothes and stuff from home."

"Give me a list. That's the last place I want you to go."

"I'd really like to keep swimming every day." She sounded timid because she knew he was going to say no. "It's…really important I keep exercising."

The frown deepened. He hadn't liked the reminder that her health—and the baby's—was at risk. His "We'll see" was terse.

How could she not bow to his judgment? After seeing Maya killed and coming so close herself today, she'd be an idiot to insist on doing whatever she wanted. Except…what were her alternatives? An aerobics video? The ones aimed at pregnant women wouldn't give her anywhere near the workout she got from swimming half a mile.

"Are you hungry?" he asked.

"Not yet."

"You ready to start, then?"

"Yes." She really needed to feel proactive to combat the helplessness.

They discussed grocery stores. She most often went to Safeway because it was closest, but also shopped at Fred Meyer because of a few products only they sold. She couldn't absolutely swear the man she'd seen didn't work in the produce section or behind the customer service counter or in the pharmacy—she didn't fill prescriptions at either store—but shook her head decisively at the idea he was a checker.

"If all he's done is see me go by pushing a cart," she argued, "how did he find out my name? I might look familiar to him, but that's all."

"He could have asked around."

"But why would he?"

"You're a beautiful woman, Lina."

She only shook her head. "Then why didn't he ever call to ask me out?"

"This might have been a while ago," Bran reminded her. "Maybe he found out you were married."

She shook her head. "I only moved here a year ago, after my divorce."

"Why here?" He sounded genuinely curious.

"I wanted to get away. Finding a new job halfway through the school year wasn't easy. The opening here was perfect." She smiled a little. "Ironically, my predecessor quit because she'd just had a baby and decided not to come back to work."

"So you'd only been here six months when we—"

Her cheeks warmed. "Yes."

"Had you been dating?"

"No. I guess a few guys asked—" she had to think back "—but I wasn't ready."

"This guy wasn't one of them?"

"No. It was a couple of the male teachers, and a guy I got talking to one day at the library."

Bran gazed at her for a long minute. Finally, he said, "I have to ask you this. It doesn't have anything to do with the bank robbery or shooting."

Warily, she waited.

"I doubt you were ever much of a drinker. You know why I was at the tavern that night. Why were you?"

Of course he'd want to know. She looked down at her gauze-wrapped hands. "My ex-husband still lives in the same town as my parents. Every so often, my mother feels compelled to give me an update on him."

Bran didn't say anything.

"I really wanted to start a family. He didn't." She gave a one-shouldered shrug. "That should have been a clue, I guess. I mean, we'd talked about it before we got married. He'd wanted kids, too, eventually. Five years later, I thought the time had come. We started fighting about it." She still felt ashamed she'd been so oblivious. "I'm sure you can guess what happened."

"He was screwing around on you."

The kindness in his voice gave her the courage to lift her head and meet his eyes. "Yep. With a friend of mine, no less. A fellow teacher."

"I can see why staying on at the same school didn't sound very appealing."

"Yes." There was a point to this. "Um, the day you and I met? Mom had let me know Madison was pregnant. His new wife. *Really* pregnant. Due any minute." She grimaced. "He wanted kids. He just didn't want them with me. All those excuses he gave were bull. While I was dreaming about starting a family, he was already sleeping with her. Somehow, hearing that—"

Bran moved faster than she'd believed possible. He stepped right over the coffee table and sat on the cushion next to her. When she tried to hide her face, he turned it back so she had to look at him.

"Be glad you *didn't* have a kid with him," he said, his voice hard. "A guy like that doesn't have it in him to be any more committed to his children than he does to his wife."

"I know you're right, but..." She shook her head.

"It hurt."

This smile might have been a little better than the last one. "Finding out Wife Number Two might have already been knocked up even before he and I split was like...like an exclamation mark. He had everything I wanted, but me? Here I am, starting all over."

"Did you want to get pregnant that night? Is that why you went to the tavern?"

Shocked by what was really an accusation, Lina jerked her face from his hand and shrank into the corner of the sofa. Away from him. "Do you really think that? I went out to pick up some guy and trick him into having unprotected sex?"

"I'm asking," he said grimly.

"No!" Being on the verge of tears made her even madder. It had to be pregnancy hormones. "I don't want to be here anymore." Still hunching away from him, she swung her feet to the floor. "Find someplace else for me to go, or I will."

"Lina. I had to ask."

"No, you really didn't." She struggled with the zipper on his sweatshirt and, finally losing patience, tugged the whole thing over her head. When she threw it, Bran snatched the sweatshirt out of the air.

"Lina, please." He sounded hoarse. "You're right. I shouldn't have said that. I just didn't like to think—" He stopped abruptly.

Even through her anger, she got it. "That it was

you only because you happened to be the one who sat beside me and started a conversation."

"Yeah. Shit."

Her shoulders slumped. "Picking up a guy never crossed my mind. I don't *do* things like that. I just wanted to get drunk, something else I never do. Doing it in public seemed more—" God, this was humiliating to admit "—melodramatic." She scrunched up her face. "Stupid."

"Like me, a cop, deciding to get drunk, also in public and despite the fact I knew I'd have to drive myself home, that I'd risk my career if I got pulled over. All because the next day was supposed to be my wedding day."

"Now that you mention it."

The crease in one cheek deepened. "You didn't have to agree."

"You just accused me of being some kind of—"

He was still close enough to put a hand over her mouth. "Don't say it. I knew better."

"How can you?" Lina said honestly. "We *don't* know each other very well."

He opened his mouth, but then thought better of whatever he'd been going to say and closed it.

"What?" she asked, suspicious.

Bran only shook his head. "We'll fix that. We're going to be spending plenty of time together from here on out."

"Because of the baby."

"Because you're staying with me."

She should have realized that he hadn't brought her here just to talk. "But…do you have a spare room?"

He quirked an eyebrow. "Not like we haven't slept in the same bed before."

Lina glared at him.

Bran didn't react. "No, I turned the second bedroom into an office. I'll sleep out here on the couch. You can have the bedroom."

"I can't take your room. Anyway, I'm smaller. I'd be comfortable on the sofa."

"No." His tone shut down any further argument. "You're pregnant. You'll take the bed."

She hesitated. "Isn't there anywhere else I could go?"

His gaze was direct and unapologetic. "Where? Anywhere you go, you could endanger someone else. I thought about my brother's place, but Tess barely survived an attempt to kill her just this spring. I can't put them in that position." He shot to his feet. "In fact, let me give you a tour."

"What?" Was there a secret compartment? A Murphy bed that would be tricky to lower? A— But she saw from his face that he was serious, so without argument she trailed him down the short hall to the door on the right, which turned out to open into a bedroom with a big bed. As with the rest of the apartment, the room was bare except for plain furnishings: a bedside lamp and clock, and another bookcase.

He bent at the foot of the bed and pulled out a tangle of metal bars and chains.

Lina blinked. *Oh.* A ladder?

"That's right," he said levelly, and she realized she'd said that aloud. "Hooks over the balcony railing. And do you know why I have this?"

Obviously, because the apartment was four stories up. But she could tell that wasn't his point, so she shook her head.

He kicked the ladder back under the bed and straightened, his eyes boring into hers. "Because Tess almost died in a fire set by the asshole who intended to kill her. Made me think. It should make *you* think."

Any protest died unspoken. She'd seen the terror on Maya's face; seen her die. Watching someone else—someone *she* had put at risk? No. Bran had the skills to protect her. And he was right; they did need to get to know each other. She'd just have to live with the panic that made her want to run from him—the same panic that had kept her from telling him about the baby as soon as she should have.

She nodded. "I understand."

"You ready to get back to work?"

"Yes." She almost apologized for flipping out, but stopped herself. She was still angry at his accusation.

He held out the sweatshirt.

Subdued, she took it, turning it right side out before she put it on. It definitely did smell like him, she decided, as it went over her head.

He walked past her and, once again, she followed obediently. Without looking at her, he sank into his chair, picking up the notepad and pen on the way. "Where do you get gas?"

She understood his retreat. And this was important. Until she could remember where she'd seen that man, she couldn't go home.

"Usually Safeway. You know, because of the discounts. But sometimes Arco."

"Do you go inside to pay at Arco?"

"No. Lately I've been thinking about it, because the price is lower if you pay cash, but then I'd have to carry cash and I hardly ever do. So far, I've paid at the pump both places. If there's an attendant at Safeway…well…I've never noticed him."

"Prescriptions."

"We could go on like this forever without doing any good," she exclaimed in frustration. "I mean, what if I bumped into the guy on the sidewalk or in a parking lot?"

"How would he have known who you were?"

"Maybe he wrote down my license plate."

"Why?"

"He was pissed. Or attracted. Take your pick. *You're* the one who suggested—"

"Let's go with the odds," he suggested, unperturbed by her outburst. "Prescriptions."

Lina sighed. "I don't have any regular ones, but I'm getting my prenatal vitamins at Walgreens."

CHAPTER SEVEN

BRAN HAD NO sooner poured himself a second cup of coffee the next morning when an irritating buzz startled him. He swore when he spilled coffee. Growling, he ran cold water over his hand before he grabbed a dish towel and finally went to the speaker.

"Yeah?"

"It's Zach. Buzz me in."

Without another word, he did. He cocked his head and heard the shower running. The knock on his door came seconds later.

Zach stomped in, scowling. "Do you ever answer your phone?"

"You know I do." He suddenly wasn't sure where it even was, an unusual state of affairs for him. Charging, that was it. "I slept in," he muttered.

"I left two messages yesterday. Texted."

Crap. He did vaguely recall ignoring his phone when it vibrated yesterday evening. He hadn't wanted to interrupt Lina or stop the flow of recollections.

"I was tied up."

His brother's gaze went to the pair of cereal bowls sitting in the sink. His eyebrows rose. "You have a woman here."

Annoyed, Bran said, "Not like you're thinking. It's Lina."

Zach smirked. "How'd you talk her into this?"

"She can't go home."

Zach frowned. "Because of the bank robbery? I thought you'd decided—"

"I decided wrong." And Bran really hated making mistakes. "Didn't you hear? Someone shot at her yesterday."

"What the—"

Bran told him what had happened as he poured them both coffee. The two men sat at the table.

"Man, she used up a lifetime of luck," his brother said, shaking his head.

Bran glared at him. "Don't say that."

"It was a figure of speech." Zach shook his head. "Was it the cargo van?"

"No. She saw only a blur as she dove for cover, but says it was gray. The two witnesses agreed it was a sedan, and kind of a beater. One of them looked for the license plate, and says it was covered. He thinks a white plastic grocery sack was tied around it."

"Which could be ripped off in about ten seconds as soon as they were out of sight of the high school."

"Yep. The driver was the shooter, too. He presumably already knew where Lina was parked, so he came up the aisle behind her so he could shoot out his driver-side window."

"He'd followed her," Zach said thoughtfully.

"Had to have."

"Not good."

"No. We talked to people using the gym and the pool, but nobody noticed a car fitting that description even though he had to be hovering somewhere."

"Most people don't pay any attention to their surroundings." Zach took a swallow of coffee. "You talk to the FBI agent?"

Bran told him what Novinski had said.

"I can see why she thinks that." Zach held up a hand before Bran could explode. "A coincidence like this might happen in a high crime neighborhood in Seattle, and that's her turf. Here, not so much. I agree you have to act on the belief that the shooter was the robber she saw."

Bran realized the shower had cut off a few minutes ago. Lina would be emerging any minute. He'd have felt compelled to warn her they weren't alone, except she wouldn't step out of the bathroom without being fully dressed down to shoes and socks anyway. Despite his optimism over the holiday, they were a long way from her relaxing that much around him.

"I'm going by her place this morning to pack

some stuff for her," he said. "I wanted to do it in full daylight so I can be damn sure no one follows me back here."

His brother scrutinized him. "What's your next step?"

Bran updated him on what he and Charlie had found from the security cameras, then went to get his notes from the night before. He handed his brother the notebook. "If you can think of anything I forgot…"

Zach flipped through the pages. "So far, you've come up with squat." He went back to the beginning and skimmed again. "Hairdresser," he said after a minute. "I know her hair is long, but she might still get it trimmed or, I don't know, lightened."

"The color is natural." Bran cleared his throat. Why did he have to say that? "But it's a good thought."

"And how about one of those places that does nails?"

Paige had gone for a mani-pedi more often than Bran washed his Camaro.

"What are the chances of her seeing a man there?"

Zach shrugged. "I guess men get theirs done, too."

A businessman or a salesman, maybe. But a bank robber?

The bathroom door opened and both men turned their heads. Lina stepped out, her eyes widening as she saw that Bran wasn't alone.

"Oh! Um, hi, Zach."

"Hey," he said. "I hear you had some more excitement yesterday."

She made a face and came toward them, wearing yesterday's maternity jeans and, he assumed, her own long-sleeve tee under the sweatshirt he'd loaned her. Her feet were bare, and her braided hair was wet. Swallowed by the oversize sweatshirt, she looked extraordinarily young and innocent, giving him a glimpse of the girl she'd been.

"I guess you need a hair dryer," he realized, hoping the huskiness in his voice went unnoticed.

"That will be on my list." She looked ruefully at their coffee. "My herbal teas, too."

"Really?" Zach sounded startled. "By *choice*?"

She chuckled. "No, I like my coffee. I *love* coffee. But I gave up caffeine for the duration."

His gaze flicked to her belly and he winced. "Pregnant women do that, huh?"

"If they're following their doctor's recommendations." She sighed and pulled out a chair. "Mine says the occasional caffeine is fine, but a good cup of coffee just makes me want more, so abstinence was easier."

"Man." Zach shook his head. "I'd better warn Tess about this."

This laugh of hers was more like a giggle, a ripple of sound that stirred Bran's body uncomfortably.

"I'm sure she knows," Lina said. "Women talk. Speaking of… If you want privacy…"

Zach shook his head. "He was telling me about your situation."

Bran frowned. "That's not why you came, though. What had you so hot and bothered?"

"I met with Mrs. Greaver yesterday, remember? I had to switch my days off with Badgley so I could do it. But you apparently don't give a—" He cleared his throat, clearly thinking better of his choice of words given Lina's presence.

"Don't accuse me of that. You offered to take my place because I'm tied up."

"Can't walk and chew gum at the same time?" his brother mocked.

Bran's jaw tightened. "Keeping Lina alive is my priority. Sheila has been dead a long time."

Zach slapped his hand on the table hard enough to make it jump. "Who are you kidding?" His tone was scathing. "I kept on with this even when Tess was threatened. Truth is, Sheila never was a priority for you. If she had been, you'd have done something a long time ago."

Bran had forgotten Lina was there, forgotten anything except his frustration with this brother who was unwilling to forgive. "You know why I didn't," he said through his teeth.

Zach's lip curled derisively. "Why did I bother to come over?"

"Goddamn it, you could just tell me what you learned—"

His brother pushed back his chair and stood. "You know what? I'll pursue this on my own." He slammed out of the apartment.

Bran tipped his head back, closed his eyes and let loose a few blistering words. Still steaming, he opened his eyes and grabbed his coffee cup. That's when he saw Lina, sitting right where she'd been, quietly watching him.

"Damn. I'm sorry."

She caught her lip in her teeth while she seemed to debate what she should say. She finally settled on, "I thought you were friends."

He grunted. "We are. Most of the time. These things just…blow up. I'd like to say it's always him, but he pushes my buttons, too."

"This isn't any of my business." She started to push her chair back.

Somehow, he clamped his mouth shut on what he wanted to say. *No, it isn't.* Because…that wasn't really true. She'd find out about Sheila and the damn investigation when—if—she married him.

Which meant he had to tell her something.

"You might as well hear about it now," he said brusquely. "We had a sister. When she was six years old, she was murdered."

Her hand still gripping the back of her chair, Lina gaped at him. It was a moment before she said softly, "Oh, no. I'm so sorry."

Bran shook his head. "It was a long time ago." Damned if he'd let this turn into a confessional. The basics were all she had to know.

Her forehead crinkled. "Sheila? That was your sister?"

"Yeah." To avoid her searching gaze, he swallowed his rapidly cooling coffee.

"But…who is Mrs. Greaver? What does that have to do with—"

"Does it matter?" he snapped.

After a long stare, she wiped all expression from her face. "Apparently not," she said coolly. "At least not to *you*."

He ground his teeth. "What's that supposed to mean?"

"You managed to convince your brother you don't care." Lina pushed the chair in and walked away.

Bran thrust his own chair out of the way and stalked after her. "You want to know every goddamn detail? Is that it?"

Lina stopped with her back to him. "She would have been my daughter's aunt," she said with quiet dignity. "But, really, that will be between her and you someday, when she's old enough for you to tell her about your family. If you'll excuse me, I'll make that list of things I need from my apartment."

She might as well demand he peel a layer of skin off if he was to have a chance at talking her into a wedding, he thought, cornered. But he had to do it. Her walking away…that wasn't going to happen.

"Come and sit down," he said hoarsely to her back. "There isn't any reason not to tell you. It's just—" Damn, his throat was closing. He thought he'd gotten past that.

Lina turned, her expression grave, eyes dark and searching. "You have a right to say no."

Frustration flared. Yeah. Sure, he did. But all he did was shake his head. "It's hard for me to talk about. That's all."

Appearing less than thrilled about coming back to the table, she did. He was wound too tight to sit while he told her about the hideous day when Zach found their baby sister naked and dead in the backyard. Bran spread his arms and gripped the counter edge, seeing another time and place, even as he remained aware of Lina's muffled sounds of distress off to one side.

"My first sight of Zach—" Remembering his

brother's face, he bowed his head, eyes closed, and fought for control.

He didn't hear Lina coming, but suddenly she was rubbing the taut muscles in his back, giving him her silent support. Fighting the need to turn around and lunge for her, hold her until the wave of pain subsided, he clenched his teeth.

Thirty seconds later, the wave receded. He straightened, aware when Lina's hand dropped away. He gave himself another few seconds, then faced her.

"I'm okay."

She read his mood enough to retreat to the table. This time, Bran managed to sit, legs stretched out, in a pretense at relaxation. He told her matter-of-factly about his parents' ugly breakup and the choices he and Zach had to make. He had dedicated his life to never feeling so helpless again.

"Fast-forward twenty-four years," he said wryly.

"What? You mean—"

"We lost contact after about a year. After that, I never heard from him or my mother until this year, when I happened to run into the new deputy coming down the hall at headquarters. Now, there was a shock. As it turned out, for both of us."

"Wow. Neither of you looked for each other?"

"I thought about it, but…" He shrugged. "I figured he'd be a stranger to me." Which Zach was, in many ways, even as he sometimes seemed so familiar.

This tension with Zach was strictly between them. Except it no longer was, entirely, or maybe never had been, Bran realized; Tess had gotten involved early on, and now there was Lina. If she was going to be his wife—and he was determined she would be—he couldn't keep family secrets from her.

So he forced himself to go on, to tell her the rest: that Zach had always believed their father killed Sheila, because he knew Dad had lied to the police about not having gotten up during the night, and because the investigators had made it so obvious *they* thought Dad was guilty. In contrast, Bran had known by the time he turned twelve that their mother was taking one lover after another, right in the bed she shared at night with her husband. Some of those men must have seen Sheila; she'd had half-day kindergarten and stuck closer to home than Zach and Bran did.

Bran had passionately believed all these years that one of his mother's lovers had admired her pretty, delicate little girl and knew which bedroom was hers. Bran had wondered how many keys to the house Mom had given out.

"Dad was too stubborn to move away even though he might have had a better life if he had. He faced people down and stayed in the house.

Even when I made detective, he didn't want me to investigate Sheila's murder. I always thought it was because he believed, like I did, Mom shared a portion of the guilt, but he still loved her. He never remarried."

Bran fell silent, remembering the grief that had never left his father. He'd lost his daughter in the most horrible way, then his wife and one of his two sons. All those years, Bran hadn't been able to understand how a man could still love the woman who had betrayed him and maybe opened the door to the monster who did that to Sheila, but Dad wouldn't hear a bad word about Bran's mother, whatever bitter things he'd said to her himself.

"When Zach came back to town and realized I was a detective here and hadn't solved the crime, he'd been sure Dad had prevented me because he thought I'd come up with evidence proving his guilt." Bran huffed out a breath. "He claims to have changed his mind, but I'm not sure I buy it."

She had a way of looking at him that made him feel as if he was gazing into a crystal ball. It was damned uncomfortable.

He told her most of the rest anyway, because if she spent any time around him and Zach, she'd hear about it eventually.

Lina winced, hearing how he and Zach had tracked down as many of their mother's former lovers as they could identify and how they'd eliminated them as suspects one by one.

He'd just think he was done, thank God, and she'd ask a question. He talked until he was close to losing his voice, expressing his anger at the inadequate records that were all the Clear Creek PD could produce, and at the one original investigator who hadn't retired but had taken offense that the Murphy boys were stepping on his toes.

Forehead crinkling, she said, "But...what if it was someone passing through town, or even a local who didn't live near you but happened to drive down your street and see Sheila playing in the yard? At night, though..." she added lamely.

"Then we'll never know who did it."

That wouldn't happen. Bran looked down to see that he'd balled his hands into fists on his thighs. "How did a stranger get in the house? How did he know which bedroom was Sheila's? He'd have woken Mom and Dad if he opened their door, or us if he'd tried upstairs. No." He shook his head. "It had to be someone who'd been in our house, knew where we slept, knew the fence in back made the yard private."

Lina shivered. "That makes sense." She studied him with that same, grave expression. "So... who did Zach talk to yesterday?"

Of course they'd circled back around to the blowup with his brother. Bran felt the burn of

resentment in his esophagus. He'd have gotten
around to all this eventually, but she had to push.
There was a really good reason he'd kept Paige
at a distance.

Which might be why she dumped me.

That reminder failed to soothe his searing resentment.

"We've moved on to former neighbors. Mrs.
Greaver's husband is dead, but she has a son who
was, I don't know, two or three years older than
me. He could have come by when his sister was
babysitting Sheila."

"A neighborhood kid."

"The investigators settled on Dad right away,
and didn't look closely at other possibilities."

She was quiet for a moment. "I think you
should go after Zach. You two need to talk."

Bran stared at her incredulously, his resentment cresting. "I haven't talked enough to sat-
isfy you? Is this some kind of test? If I don't go
make nice, I fail?"

Lina shook her head and pushed back from the
table. "Do what you want. I'll make you a list."

This time, he didn't try to stop her.

"You do that," he muttered, after she'd disappeared into the bedroom.

A sick feeling told him she was right; he did
need to clear the air with his brother. But damned
if he'd tell her that.

What he needed was a break from her, from the sexual tension that probably explained some of the frustration and anger that choked him. From the way she left him feeling like his guts were hanging out.

From his pitiful desire to tell her anything, if she'd just agree to marry him.

LINA HEARD THE sound of the key turning just as her stomach started to complain. Dread and hunger didn't mix well. She wished she'd eaten before Bran returned.

Unfortunately, the door opened while she was lying flat on her back on his living room floor. She hadn't managed to sit up when he appeared, arms laden and pulling her large suitcase behind him.

"Hey. Tipped over and couldn't get up?"

His expression was guarded. Or was that apprehensive?

Framed in the doorway, he was the sexiest man she'd ever seen. Disheveled hair—had he ever combed it today?—broad shoulders, sharp blue eyes. The awareness infuriated her, given the way he'd lashed out at her before leaving.

Weren't they supposed to be getting to know each other? His suggestion? Right. Sure.

It occurred to her that maybe they were. She'd

learned that having to acknowledge his own painful emotions turned Bran Murphy mean.

Flushing under his gaze now, she sat up with considerably less grace than she used to have. "Doing some exercises." Her eyes went to the white bag dangling from one of his hands. "You brought lunch?"

"Yep. Didn't know if you indulge in junk food, but it sounded good to me."

He had to do something nice *now*?

"I surrender occasionally." And, oh, it smelled good.

Lina waited until he'd detoured to the kitchen before rolling to her knees and using the coffee table as a crutch to help her get up.

"Cheeseburgers and fries," he said, setting the bag on the table. "Milk shakes."

While he took the suitcase into the bedroom, she explored the contents of the bags and distributed the food. Lina had already unwrapped her burger by the time he returned.

"Was my place okay?" she asked, before taking a big bite. Apparently, they were going to ignore the fight, if you could call it that when it had been one-sided. Which was probably better, given that she had no choice but to stay with him.

"Nobody had broken in, if that's what you mean. But why would they, if you're not there?"

He frowned. "Unless… Is there any chance this guy could be in a photo you've taken?"

"I can't imagine. I don't take many, and these days, only with my phone. So I post pictures on Facebook, or email them. I hardly ever print one."

She stuck the straw into her milk shake and ate a fry.

Sitting across from her, Bran didn't move. Lina picked up her burger again.

"I've never told anyone before," he said abruptly, voice gritty.

Startled, she looked up. "You mean, about your sister?"

He gave a single, hard nod.

"But…" Shaking her head in disbelief, she said, "How is that possible?"

His shoulders moved. "My father knew. We didn't talk about it. Neighbors and friends knew. Later, there was no reason to tell anyone."

"Not even Paige?" She couldn't help remembering what Tess had said about how closed off he was.

"No." He took a deep breath, his eyes never leaving hers. "I'd…put it out of my mind. As much as I could. Until Zach showed up out of the blue."

"And he knew, too."

"Yes."

Her heart had taken to beating fast. *I'm the first*

person he has ever told. He'd said it was difficult. She just hadn't had any idea how difficult.

"Why me?" she finally asked.

A nerve twitched in his cheek. "You're the mother of my baby."

Lina sighed. Not the explanation she wanted, but she'd accept it for now. She nodded and bent to her milk shake.

Bran took a couple bites before saying, "I stopped by Zach's."

"Seriously?"

"Yeah." He grimaced. "He apologized. I think he was embarrassed."

"Of course he was."

His eyebrows rose.

"Throwing a temper tantrum like that was childish."

"Tess was standing in the background, arms crossed, giving him the laser stare."

Lina laughed. "I don't believe that."

"She can be a tough broad, don't kid yourself." He sounded as if he admired his sister-in-law. "She was definitely giving him the look."

"The look?"

His mouth quirked. "The same one you gave me when you ordered me to go talk to him."

"I did not order you! I...suggested."

This was one of the first laughs she'd heard

from him. She could grow to love the sound and what it did to that hard, angular face.

"Uh-huh," was all he said.

She sucked on her straw, then reached for the fries. "So? Did he find out anything good?"

"Maybe. Mrs. Greaver was tight-lipped about her son. Sounds like he might be a disappointment to her, but Zach didn't think that was all of it. He said the fireplace mantel was crowded with pictures, but Rob was absent except for some family photos when he was a kid."

"That might not have anything to do with your sister."

"Maybe not, but Mama Greaver declined to be party to our investigation. If the police thought my father did it, that was good enough for her. Zach says she got uncomfortable when he asked about Rob, even just what he's doing these days."

"Guaranteeing that you two will consider him seriously as a possible suspect." Lina had mixed feelings. "The poor woman was trying to protect her son."

"The poor woman?" Bran's teeth showed when he leaned forward. "Is that any excuse if she suspects he likes little girls?"

"No, but...it would be hard. That's all I'm saying. Parents are, or should be, wired to protect their children, don't you think?" She saw where he was looking, and realized she had covered the firm mound that was now her waistline with both hands in an unconscious gesture of, yes, protection.

"Yeah." Bran's voice had softened, become gruff. He met her eyes again. "I do get that."

He was quiet, leaving her to wonder if he'd just been struck by the hard reality that he would soon be a parent himself.

Once so sure she could do this alone, Lina discovered at that moment how much she hoped Bran really would be in it with her for the long-term, and not only out of a rigid sense of duty and honor. This was a man willing to admit he'd been wrong. And while he hadn't exactly apologized, he'd come close enough for her.

She was bundling up the wrappings from their lunch when Bran said, in his usual, detached way, "I have a few more questions. Possibilities of where you might have seen the bank robber."

Lina could think about things she'd rather do, but she only nodded. She *needed* to remember.

WATCHING HER MOVING around the kitchen, Bran wished like hell they could take the rest of the day off. Pretend they were a normal couple.

Spend the afternoon in bed.

Not happening. But he should count his blessings. Lina was more forgiving than he deserved.

Even the act of pulling out a chair and sitting was graceful when she did it.

Seeing her expectant gaze, he asked, "Do you go to a salon or spa?"

"No, I haven't gone to any kind of spa since I moved here. I take care of my nails myself, and Maya—" her breath hitched "—always trimmed my hair."

"I'm sorry," he said gently. "You two were close, weren't you?"

Her reply was pained. "We met because I had a boy in my class last year whom she paid to mow her lawn. She saw some bruises on him and convinced him to talk to her. It was a bullying situation. He told her I was the coolest teacher, so we sat down to map out a strategy and I went with him to talk to the principal and counselor. After that, she invited me over for lunch and we just clicked. I'd already made friends here, mostly with other teachers, but they were all married, some of them had kids." This smile was small and crooked, reminding him of the jackass ex who'd hurt her. "Between work and family," she added, "they didn't have much time. Maya and I were both free to do things together."

He asked if she'd gotten involved in other situations like that. She might have barely seen an older brother, an uncle, a friend of the family at the house when she went to talk to a student's parents, but she shook her head even before he finished.

"I meet with parents at the school," she said firmly. "Always. Because this isn't that big a town, I've run into parents shopping or at the movie theater or whatever, but…" She stopped. "I don't remember meeting him that way. Truthfully—" she looked beseechingly at him "—I'm not convinced I ever did meet him. It feels more like the kind of encounter you dismiss right away."

"Car salesman?" he thought to ask.

"I already owned my Kia. I drove myself out here from Minnesota. It's sort of a stretch to think he's from back home and we just happened to end up in the same place, halfway across the country. And, no, I didn't have a stalker back home."

Bran fixated on part of what she'd said, his protective side kicking in. "You made that drive in the dead of winter by yourself? Didn't your parents object?"

She raised her eyebrows. "I wasn't eighteen and just leaving for college, you know. I was thirty-one years old. We have a lot more snow back there than we do here, so I'm experienced driving in it."

"Your parents didn't have anything to say about that?" Bran almost wished he and Lina weren't having a girl. He'd be scared shitless every time he had to take his eyes off her.

"My father wanted me to sell the car and buy a new one when I got here. Actually, he tried to convince me to live at home until I could find a job a whole lot closer to them. That made me all the more determined to get away."

Bran could understand that. A bigger mystery was why he had made a life here in Clear Creek after his sister's death, considering the attitude of people who should have been his father's friends. *And yet*, Bran thought uneasily, *here I am*.

It disturbed him to think Lina, in striking out on her own, had shown more independence than he had. Did she wonder why he'd stayed in this backwater county, or did she just assume it was all he knew and it felt safe and comfortable?

If so, she'd be wrong. He'd left for college, and then after the academy started his career with the Seattle PD. Originally he'd taken the job here because of Dad's declining health. But even after burying his father, he'd never considered moving away again. He had never really analyzed why, and *that* bothered him now.

He'd been having all kinds of unwelcome epiphanies since he met Lina Jurick, it occurred to him. And he thought he wanted to marry her?

But even this new sense of vulnerability couldn't shake his decision. She was right for him, and with her carrying his baby, they were already a family. He'd either learn to deflect her or he'd resign himself to having his hidden depths filtered until they became so crystal clear, even he'd be able to see right through them.

"We have the rest of the day," Lina said.

Crap. He knew what she was thinking. "You want to go swimming."

The hope in her eyes was timid, but there. "You said maybe."

He just hadn't said no. *Hell, no. Are you crazy? No.*

But, Jesus, what if *not* swimming endangered her and the baby? He frowned. The creep couldn't stake out the high school swimming pool ten hours a day. He wouldn't be looking for Lina in the Camaro.

Bran still wasn't happy about the idea, but…

"Yeah," he said gruffly. "We can go." Even though going to the high school, where she'd already been attacked once, went against his every instinct.

Her face lit up. "Really? Do you swim?"

"Not well enough to swim laps. I need to stay aware anyway. I'll watch."

Shadowed by the reminder, her expression dimmed. "You really think you need to be on guard while I'm in the pool?"

"Nah." He half smiled. "I was trying to get out of embarrassing myself."

Lina giggled. "Oh, for heaven's sake! Wouldn't it feel good?"

"The hot tub would," he admitted. Seeing her in a bathing suit. That would feel good.

"I'll go grab my stuff," she said eagerly.

"Aren't you supposed to give it an hour after a meal before you go in the water?"

Lina subsided, making a face at him. "I suppose. Fine. I'll go see what you brought for me."

"You mean, check to see what I forgot?"

She offered a saucy smile. "Now, what would make you think I'm that critical?"

Just like that, his body hardened. He needed to kiss her. *Now.*

She went still, her eyes dilating.

In silence, they stared at each other.

CHAPTER EIGHT

BRAN FLAILED HIS way up and back half a dozen times, thankful he wasn't the only one in the pool whose strokes couldn't be mistaken for Michael Phelps's. He remembered Lina telling him she'd swam competitively, which explained why she sliced through the water with such effortless efficiency even with the extra weight she was hauling.

This was his second visit with her. She'd been so happy after swimming yesterday, so obviously invigorated, he'd agreed to this evening, too, even though he wasn't any happier about it than he had been yesterday.

Monday was one of his usual days off, as long as he wasn't tied up in a particularly intense investigation. This time, staying home hadn't been an option, between the double slaying during the bank robbery and the threat to Lina, never mind the rest of his caseload. And maybe that was just as well, given how hard it was to keep his hands off her. After yesterday's prolonged proximity, some distance today had seemed smart.

He stopped at the shallow end, shook his head, spraying water, and scanned the room. Two older women appeared from the locker room, the teenage lifeguard was flirting with a girl who didn't look more than about thirteen and a man who'd been in the lane next to Lina's had disappeared. No—that had to be the back of his dark head, appearing above the edge of the hot tub. All was well.

Bran had been disappointed to learn that, because of her pregnancy, Lina couldn't join him in the hot tub after her laps. Yesterday, he'd grabbed a few minutes in it when he thought she might be nearly done. If he sat so he could still see the pool, it seemed safe enough.

The added benefit was being able to watch her rise from the pool and walk across the deck toward him in a racing-style suit that fit her like a second skin. Yesterday, during the drive home, she'd ruefully confessed that it wasn't a maternity suit, and she was stretching out the fabric enough, she'd have to throw it away when she outgrew it. At the moment, it looked more than fine, however. Her body was everything he remembered and more.

Her legs and arms were still long and taut with a swimmer's muscles. The summer's tan was gone. Her already generous breasts were bigger, he thought, along with that ripe swell of belly.

Damned if she didn't turn him on as much now as she had before.

Time for the hot tub. He levered himself out of the pool, checked automatically to see where Lina was and strolled over to join the one other guy already lounging in the bubbling water.

He'd have liked to close his eyes and lay back, but couldn't let himself relax his vigilance. Lina was probably safe in here, but it wasn't in his nature to count on it. So even as the hot tub jets loosened his tight muscles, he scanned the deck, eyed the wall of glass looking for movement beyond it, automatically assessed everyone coming and going from the locker rooms.

He was glad to see Lina finally duck under lane ropes and take hold of the ladder. He doubted she bothered with a ladder normally, but her new bulk had to have changed how she did a lot of things.

Water streamed from her as she appeared, darkening her hair, confined in a single, fat braid. She gleamed, all that pale skin and rich curves. Her gaze went straight to him, which meant she'd noticed when he left the pool.

She stopped close enough he could have touched her pretty feet. "I so wish I could hop in there."

"Hop?" he teased.

That earned him a wrinkled nose. "Climb *carefully* in there." She sighed. "Take your time. I don't mind waiting if I get ready first."

He nodded, but had no intention of letting her emerge out front alone.

Like the day before, he had to take a minute to let his body's reaction to her near-nudity subside. Living with her and not making a move was killing him. He wondered if she had any idea how much he wanted her.

He wasn't 100 percent sure what was holding him back. Yeah, the fear of making her uncomfortable given that she had to depend on him contributed. He was chagrined to acknowledge that it was also his own fear of being rejected. From the way she looked at him sometimes—like yesterday—he believed she felt the attraction, too, as much as she had the night they met.

Trouble was, nothing between them was simple anymore. She'd had to deal with the shock of learning she was pregnant only to have him essentially accuse her of using him because she *wanted* to be pregnant. Not smart on his part. The damned wedding invitation and the timing of that night still stung when she thought about it, too, he knew without asking. Did she think he'd imagined she was Paige when they made love? Was he sure himself he hadn't been taking some subconscious form of revenge on Paige for dumping him?

Now, there'd be an irony, given how immensely grateful he now was that Paige hadn't gone through with the wedding. Which sent him back to yesterday's reflections on how poorly he understood his own deeper motives.

At least he could get out of the hot tub now, the depressing reflections having taken care of his problem. Bran showered quickly and wasted no time getting dressed. As a result, he had to wait a good ten minutes for her, no surprise given that she had to dry that mass of hair.

When she emerged from the locker room, for a moment he saw only her. Her glorious hair hung loose over a tunic that clung to her curves more than she probably imagined. As he watched, she shrugged on a parka that clearly would no longer meet in front.

"You're beautiful," he said roughly, catching her hand.

Her eyes widened. "I'm more than a little pregnant, in case you haven't noticed."

"I've noticed." He cleared his throat. "Got everything?"

"I…" Her gaze shied from his. "Yes."

"All right." He led her to the door, wishing the lighting was better in the parking lot. He had parked illegally as close to the entrance as he could, leaving a sign on the dashboard identifying the vehicle as law enforcement. "You know the drill."

Lina nodded. He tucked her close to his left

side, angling to keep her between him and the wall of the building until they reached the Camaro. There he unlocked and hustled her in before going around to the driver's side himself.

The arrival and departure were the part of the outing he had dreaded tonight. Yesterday, he'd had the advantage of daylight. Tonight, he was all too aware that someone could have waited for them to walk out, backlit through the glass doors, or have ducked between parked cars preparing to shoot as he drove past. But damn it, he'd swear no one had followed him, and how else could anyone know where she was?

In the rearview mirror, he saw movement.

"Take off the seat belt," he said suddenly. "Get down."

She fumbled for the release. With a hand on her back, he pushed her forward even as he accelerated with a squeal of tires. Lina hunched down, letting him use both hands on the wheel to circle the perimeter of the parking lot like a race car driver.

"What's wrong?" Her voice came out strangled. "Do you see someone?"

Christ—with only one road in and out, setting up an ambush would be a breeze. *What was I thinking?* Headlights came on behind him in the lot, somewhere midway down an aisle. Ahead... the beams of his own headlights found nothing.

He drove tensely, gaze switching from the road ahead to the rearview mirror to side mirrors. Only when they approached a major cross street did his muscles loosen. The light turned green as they approached, and he swung a right.

"Okay," he said. "You can sit up."

Lina groaned and straightened.

"Seat belt," he said.

She obeyed. "What happened?" Her voice was taut with anxiety. "Did you see something?"

"I thought I did." His fingers flexed on the leather-wrapped steering wheel. "Coming here is stupid. Open season."

"How can it be? They don't know where I'm staying, they don't know your car! What do you think, they're just staking out the high school?"

"It's possible." Pretty damned unlikely, but he wasn't about to admit as much.

"Really? Twenty-four/seven, on the off chance I show up?" Disbelief seemed to be warming up her temper.

"It's possible," he repeated. "The pool is the one place they know you've come. You're not home. Where else are they going to find you?"

"You're saying I can't go swimming again."

He hesitated, glancing at her profile under a passing headlight. The stakes were high either way—her health or her life. "I don't know. Let me think about it."

"What am I going to do if you can't find them?" She didn't look at him; he wasn't 100 percent sure she was even talking to him. "Maybe I should go home."

"To your apartment? The hell you're—"

"No. I mean home. Minnesota."

His hands tightened convulsively on the steering wheel until it creaked. He needed her to stay here, where he could protect her, where he'd *know* she was safe.

And, damn it, home should be here, where he was, not somewhere in the Midwest.

"If they know anything about you, they could find out where you came from. Where your parents live. What if they were to follow you, Lina?"

She clutched the belt in a fist where it crossed her torso above her belly. "Do you really believe they'd do that?"

"I don't know." That, at least, was honest. "As time passes, they may relax and decide you can't identify him. This soon… I'm guessing they're pretty focused on eliminating you as a threat."

Belatedly, he realized how brutally blunt that was. She didn't look at him.

"Maybe I'm being paranoid," he said, more quietly. "That goes with my job, too. But…"

"Better safe than sorry?"

"Yeah," he said regretfully. "Something like that."

She didn't say anything, which left him worrying about what she was thinking. Cops had a really high divorce rate, and there were good reasons. The unpredictable hours, the inability to talk about what they did, the high incidence of PTSD and alcoholism were all factors.

Paige hadn't seen Bran working except for their initial meeting, when he'd been at the hospital in Mount Vernon to talk to a gunshot victim. She didn't ask about what he did in any given day, he didn't offer to tell her. Long term, he thought now, they'd have been living together like two strangers.

That wouldn't fly with Lina, obviously. She had a way of seeing right through his defenses. If she didn't like what she saw…hell. How was he supposed to deal with that?

He took a couple of unnecessary turns in town to be absolutely sure no one was behind him before going home. After parking, he once again had her wait until he came around to help her out, then hustled her into the lobby and used his body to shield her from the wall of windows.

He hated when they had to wait for the damn elevator.

This wasn't the kind of place to raise a kid

anyway. He needed to start thinking about buying a house.

Once in the apartment, she went straight to the bathroom, undoubtedly to hang up her suit and towel. He hoped she wouldn't go straight to bed, although he wouldn't be surprised if she did. She obviously wasn't interested in talking to him.

Bran mumbled an expletive and scrubbed a hand over his face. He hated this uncertainty. Not knowing for sure how she felt about him. What she thought. He wanted everything tied up. A ring on her finger, the right to claim her as his. The idea of her, down the line, meeting some other man, starting to date, even marrying... The worry ate at the lining of his stomach like acid.

Lina emerged from the bathroom and came back to the living room, looking at him in surprise. "Is something wrong?"

"No."

"Do you want me to hang up your suit?"

"I can do it," he said grumpily.

"Okay." She went past him into the galley kitchen. "I'm going to make a cup of tea. Do you want something?"

Her. That was what he wanted.

"Coffee would keep me awake. I might have a beer."

When he came back from the bathroom, she had set a bottle of beer out on the table for him, and was pouring boiling water into a mug. Her herbal tea smelled okay; the box said it was orange-spice. She'd offered him a sip yesterday, though, and it tasted like barely-flavored hot water to him.

He had discovered that she was always cold. Her hands were almost always chilly when he held one. She rarely went barefoot around the apartment, which suggested her feet were cold, too. When he wore a sweatshirt or a long-sleeve T-shirt, she'd wear the same, add another layer and tug a fleece throw over herself, too, when she sat on the couch. He didn't own such a thing, but it had been on the list she'd given him: *Red fleece throw on back of couch.*

Everything on her list had been exactly where she'd said it was. His place was neat because he didn't own much, hers because she was organized. Hey, at least neither of them was a slob. They had something in common.

Along with a baby.

And he could warm her feet and hands at night. Volunteering would be no hardship.

He sat in his recliner, her in what had become her usual spot at the end of the couch. She kicked off her shoes and sat cross-legged, nursing the cup of tea.

"This can't go on forever," she said, her gaze direct.

Forever was exactly what he had in mind, but

he suspected she wasn't ready to hear that. And… what exactly did she mean by *this*? Getting shot at? Or living with him?

"I forgot to tell you that the artist can meet with you tomorrow afternoon," he told her. *See? We're doing something.* "I'll bring her here rather than having you come into the station."

"Oh," Lina breathed in what sounded like dismay. "I'd almost forgotten." She reached for the throw and pulled it over herself. "What if I don't remember enough? It's been days now, and I only caught the one glimpse anyway. It's not like I have any kind of artist's eye." Anxiety seeped from her every word.

"Do your best. I think you're going to be surprised. This artist has a gift. I've only had occasion to use her a couple of times, but I've seen other sketches of hers. She's a genius with traumatized children, some of whom are barely old enough to speak. Somehow she worms enough out of them to come up with a portrait so accurate, the sight of it throws them back into terror." Which, come to think of it, might not be the note he'd meant to strike.

"You're saying I might scare myself?"

"I'm saying this could be the break we need."

Her forehead wrinkled. "Will you hand it out to the media?"

"Let's wait and see how good it is." He had

other reservations, but decided not to share those. He hesitated before saying what else he was thinking, but then went ahead. "My hope is that when you see the face looking back at you, it might spark your memory."

"Of why he looked familiar," she said slowly.

"Right."

"Okay. I'll do my best." Her expression seemed to suddenly turn inward. "I don't know if you'd be interested, but…well…the baby is being really active right now." She regarded him shyly. "You could, well, feel her move, if you'd like."

"Yeah." Clearing his throat did nothing to unclog the emotions crowding him. He circled the coffee table, set down his mug and held out his hand, not quite sure where he ought to place it.

Lina lowered the fleece throw to her lap, then lifted her shirt, baring the pale swell. She took his hand and opened it, placing it over her belly. Surprised at how hard her stomach was, he waited, not breathing.

Something squirmed beneath his palm. Blinking, he lifted his head to meet her eyes. She smiled. Her whole belly bobbed, as if the baby had done a somersault.

Good God, Bran thought, in a kind of awe; maybe it had.

No, maybe *she* had.

"Having this happen inside you must feel really strange."

That soft, incredibly gentle smile still curved her mouth. "Yes and no. It makes me very aware there's a whole separate person in there. I don't suppose it's all that different from carrying a baby in a snuggly against your body."

"No, but—" He shook his head. Probably he should remove his hand, but he couldn't make himself. The next movement was more subtle, something passing beneath the surface of the water. His awareness that this was a baby, *his* baby, made the sensation incredible. "How do you sleep?"

"She does get active when I'm relaxed. I think my walking around rocks her, so she goes to sleep. I'm told sleep for me gets to be more of a challenge the bigger she gets. Eventually, she'll be punching and kicking me. I haven't felt hiccups yet, either, which happens."

"You have three more months."

"Not quite." She paused. "Unlike most people, I know exactly when I got pregnant."

Yeah, she did.

"I keep track. Tomorrow, I'll be at exactly twenty-seven weeks. So I do have ten or eleven weeks to go, if I make it full term."

Jolted, he said, "You might not?"

"Well…if my blood pressure becomes a real

issue, the doctor might decide at some point to induce labor." While he was still reeling from that, she gave him a small lecture on pregnancy and what was still to come. He was blown away to learn that the fetus was already fourteen or fifteen inches long.

"She probably only weighs a couple of pounds, though. Maybe a little more." Lina looked ruefully down at herself. "She takes up more space than she should."

Since he hadn't felt any more movement, Bran reluctantly removed his hand. Lina immediately tugged her shirt down and lifted the throw back up to her chin.

"Thank you," he said huskily.

"Yes, well…" She drew the last word out as she sneaked a glance at him, her shyness resurfacing.

That bothered him until he reminded himself how very intimate they'd become on one level, while having spent so little time together. She'd only come back into his life…five days ago? Was that all?

"Well?" he prompted. Probably he should go back to his chair, but he liked sitting close enough to see the fine texture of her skin, the way her lashes curled, the striations of color in her eyes.

"I was leading into an invitation," she said.

He sat back. Was she actually…

"I don't know if you're interested or…or can

get away, but I have a doctor's appointment on Wednesday at ten. You could hear the baby's heartbeat."

Ah. A doctor's appointment.

"You're not driving yourself," he reminded her, ignoring the flare of mutiny on her face. "But I'd like to come anyway." He stared halfway down the fleece throw to where he decided the swell of her pregnancy had to be. *A heartbeat. Damn.* "How often do you go?"

"Monthly, at this stage. I think weekly the last month, at least."

"Okay." And he'd be at every one of them with her.

"I'll be taking childbirth classes, too. The session lasts six weeks, and they have evening classes."

Was that an invitation, too? "Are they just for mothers?"

She shook her head. "We're encouraged to bring a partner to be a coach. The father, or...or a friend. I'd asked Maya, but—" Her voice broke. "If you do it, you'd have to stay for the birth. If you think—"

"Yeah." God, now he sounded hoarse. "Of course I want to do it. You couldn't keep me away."

"Well, good. I mean, we haven't talked about